AGENT ARTHUR'S JUNGLE JOURNEY

Martin Oliver

Illustrated by

Paddy Mounter

Designed by
Paddy Mounter, Kim Blundell and Brian Robertson

Series Editor: Gaby Waters

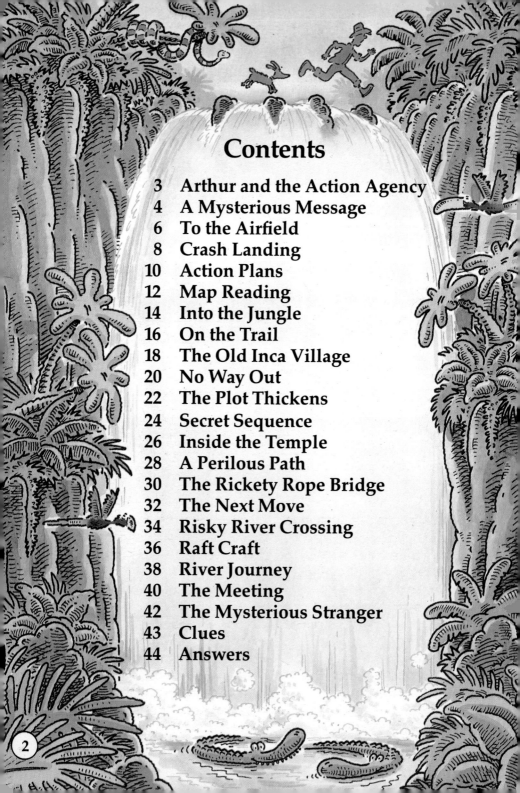

Contents

Arthur and the Action Agency

The Action Agency is a world wide undercover organization dedicated to fighting crime and solving mysteries. Supremely successful, the Agency lives up to its motto, *Search, Solve and Survive*, by operating a "go anywhere, do anything" service.

Arthur is the newest and youngest Action Agent and this book follows his first three missions. Arthur was recruited by his uncle, Jake Sharpe.

Jake is the founder and brains of the Agency. He is an elusive figure and a master of disguise, rarely seen but always respected.

You can take part in Arthur's adventures by solving the fun puzzles that appear on almost every page. Clues to the answers and vital information lurk in the pictures and the words. If you get stuck, you will find extra clues and the answers at the end of each story.

A Mysterious Message

Agent Arthur was sitting in a small office of the Action Agency. But there wasn't much action going on. In fact, except for Arthur and his dog Sleuth, no one had walked through the door for weeks and weeks.

It was summer and Arthur had been left minding the office while his Uncle Jake was away on a top secret mission. His uncle was often away for weeks, months and sometimes years on end. Meanwhile, Arthur stayed put.

Arthur was reading a comic book, dreaming about having adventures like Uncle Jake, when CRASH . . . something hurtled through the window and whistled past his left ear. He dived for cover.

Ten seconds later, Arthur peered out from behind the desk. Papers were scattered everywhere. Among them was a half-brick. Sleuth sniffed the brick warily, while Arthur cautiously removed a piece of paper wrapped round it. He saw strange signs scrawled on it – the unmistakeable symbols of the Agency Action Code.

What does the message say?

MISSING

Jane Printz, the school-
girl photographer, has
disappeared in the South
American jungle while
photographing the rare
Orchid Narcotica

Jane Printz

CROOKFAX

Name:
HENRIK HITMAN

Hired assassin
This man is
and will sh
Last seen in

CROOKFAX

Name:
RICK J.
ELDT.

CROOKFAX

Name:
EL PAUNCHO,
also called 'The Boss'

Master criminal. Suspected
links with notorious
'SPIDER' organization.

MON 16

5

To the Airfield

Arthur looked outside. The stone-thrower was nowhere to be seen.

This was it. Action! Arthur studied his map and eagerly pulled on a jacket.

He crammed a helmet on his head and raced Sleuth downstairs.

He spun round and spotted the base. They sneaked closer and keeping under cover, circled round the perimeter fence.

"What's going on?" thought Arthur, scanning the base suspiciously. "We must get on to the plane to find out."

They leapt onto the bike. Arthur pedalled and the motor choked into life.

Sleuth hung on as they zoomed down busy streets and roared out of town.

At last, Arthur stopped to recheck the map. He felt a tap on his back.

But how? Then Arthur spotted a gap in the fence. They could crawl through it safely, but they still had to get past the mean-looking guards without being spotted.

Find a safe route onto the plane.

Crash Landing

A rthur and Sleuth sneaked aboard the plane. Suddenly the door slammed shut behind them.

The plane's engines roared. Arthur and Sleuth stared out of the window in horror. They were moving.

Arthur hung on to a heavy wooden crate as the plane rattled and jolted along the bumpy runway.

Sleuth watched as Arthur shouted and banged on the cockpit door. It was no good. After a few minutes Arthur slumped down beside Sleuth.

"We'd better get comfortable," he said. "It might be a long flight."

Sleuth snorted in disgust as the plane flew on into the night.

Suddenly Arthur woke up. Sleuth was still dozing, but something was wrong.

The plane shook violently and began to nose-dive with one engine ablaze.

There was just time to wake Sleuth and get into emergency landing positions . . .

Arthur came to, waist-high in debris and seeing stars. With a start he remembered what had happened.

Where was Sleuth? Arthur spotted a familiar ear and dug him out of the wreckage. He was dazed, but OK.

They searched for the pilot. Arthur and Sleuth scrambled through the fuselage into the cockpit. It was empty, except for a large stripy snake that hissed and slithered.

Where were they? Arthur peered out of a hole in the smashed windshield. On all sides he could see a thick green jungle of trees, vines and spiky bushes. He gulped. They were alone, somewhere in a dense, tropical rainforest.

Action Plans

Arthur thought back to his Basic Training and knew immediately what to do. He must send a rescue message. But the radio was beyond repair.

Arthur leapt down from the plane. Sleuth stuck his nose out of the cabin to examine the crash site and barked angrily at a vulture circling overhead.

"Never fear," said Arthur, as he began cutting and gathering wood for fires. "We'll move into Plan Two – ground-to-air signals."

Arthur charged through the wreckage, making flags, laying out messages and shifting huge pieces of reflective metal.

"Finished at last," said Arthur, thinking how proud his Action Training Instructor would be. "Now we wait to be rescued."

Meanwhile, Sleuth was nosing about in the cockpit. He barked loudly and bounced out of the plane carrying a big black briefcase.

"Can't you see I'm busy being lookout?" Arthur asked, grumpily dumping out the case.

"This is useless," he said, waving a piece of paper covered in unusual writing. "Unless … unless … it's in code!"

Can you decode the message?

DINM LONTROC NLAP A, LIT AV TQUIPMENE DNA SUPPLIES   YEADR ROF NRANSPORTATIOT NO YONDAM MROF EHT
DLO DIRFIELA, MIA ROF GANDINL PTRIS TA IE, NHET DROC EEP OT EASB TA 1H AIV DARKEM LRAIT, EILF EALSF
TLIGHF NLAP, NI EASC FO YMERGENCE, LAIB TUO DNA TONTACC   EASB, ON EESCUR STTEMPTA   LILW EB EADM, EHEST
SRDERO ERA DSSUEI YB EHT   SOSB DNA TUSM EB DBEYED   TA   LLA SOSTC,

Map Reading

Arthur realized that they were on their own, with no hope of rescue . . . This was his big chance! Now he could use his Action Agency Training to pit his wits against whatever dangers he might encounter in the hostile jungle.

"Being intrepid Action Agents, we will investigate any suspicious goings-on at the base," Arthur said bravely. "But first we must find our position on this map."

Arthur knew that he could pinpoint their position, if only he could see some landmarks.

But how? They were hemmed in by thick jungle on all sides. Arthur sprang into action. He took a deep breath and scrambled up a steep, rocky hill, with trees growing on the summit.

At last he reached the top and peered through the trees. Sleuth was just a worried-looking dot down below, but Arthur could see for miles around. He pulled a map and compass out of his pockets.

Where are Arthur and Sleuth? Can you find the base?

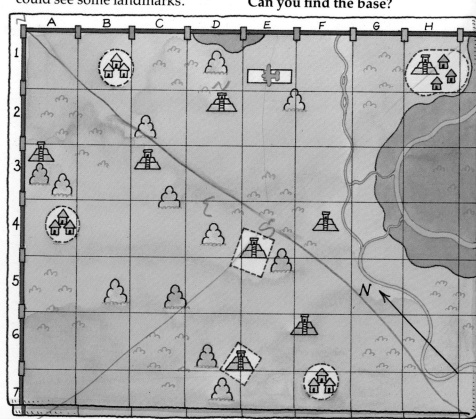

Into the Jungle

Arthur clambered back down to Sleuth and they hunted through the plane for useful equipment to make up a survival kit. Soon they were ready for the trek into the dense jungle.

Arthur strode forward, firmly gripping the handle of his machete. He hacked through the thick leaves and vines that barred their path. Huge trees towered over them and ear-splitting monkey calls shattered the silence.

They stumbled over fallen trees and waded through rotting leaves. Arthur looked back as the plane disappeared behind some spiky bushes. The jungle swallowed them up. He whistled to cheer himself up. Sleuth joined in with a loud growl.

From all around came rustling and slithering noises. Green eyes glinted menacingly at them. But there was no time to wonder about what was lurking in the undergrowth, as large raindrops began to splash down through the trees. Within minutes Arthur and Sleuth were soaked, but still they trudged on through hordes of hungry mosquitoes.

"Over there," gasped Arthur, as the rain stopped at last. "We'll rest for a bit."

They slipped and slid towards a tree trunk. Suddenly Arthur caught sight of something very unusual. He sprinted towards it, just as Sleuth barked a warning.

What has Arthur spotted?
What has Sleuth spotted?

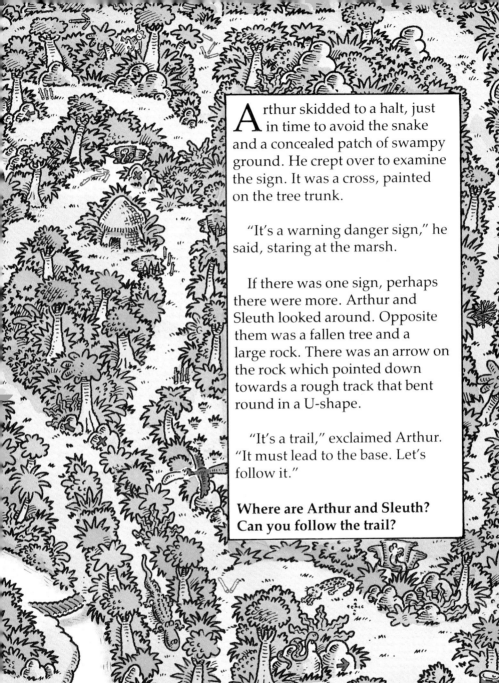

Arthur skidded to a halt, just in time to avoid the snake and a concealed patch of swampy ground. He crept over to examine the sign. It was a cross, painted on the tree trunk.

"It's a warning danger sign," he said, staring at the marsh.

If there was one sign, perhaps there were more. Arthur and Sleuth looked around. Opposite them was a fallen tree and a large rock. There was an arrow on the rock which pointed down towards a rough track that bent round in a U-shape.

"It's a trail," exclaimed Arthur. "It must lead to the base. Let's follow it."

Where are Arthur and Sleuth? Can you follow the trail?

The Old Inca Village

The trail led up a steep hill and ended abruptly at a stone wall. Below them was an old Inca village. This was the base they were searching for!

The smell of cooking came towards them. Sleuth's stomach began to rumble. He was just about to leap over the wall when he felt a hand on his collar.

"Get down Sleuth," Arthur hissed, as he stared at the armed men in the village. "Whatever they're doing here, I don't like the look of it."

Arthur's eyes narrowed. One of the men looked familiar. Arthur was sure he had seen him before.

Which man does Arthur recognize?

19

No Way Out

Arthur and Sleuth ducked out of sight and crept back into the jungle.

"Let's wait until dark and then move in," whispered Arthur. "But we must be careful."

He stepped forward. Suddenly a rope fastened round his ankle and he was hoisted up into the air. Everything went black.

We have ways of dealing with spies. Take him away.

When Arthur opened his eyes, he was lying on the ground, his head throbbing. He tried to stand up, but couldn't. His hands and feet were securely bound with strong rope.

A dark shadow loomed over him and Arthur stared up at the short, ugly figure of El Pauncho. Arthur didn't like his face, or the sound of what he was saying.

But there was no time to worry. Arthur was picked up by two guards who carried him through the village and threw him into a dingy hut.

Arthur's brain whirred. What was Pauncho doing in the jungle? Where was Sleuth? But before he could think straight, the hut began spinning and Arthur's head hit the floor.

Ouch!

It was dark when Arthur woke up. He blinked quickly to get used to the moonlight and staggered to his feet. No prison hut could hold an Action Agent. He must escape, but how? The walls were thick and there was a chunky lock on the door.

Arthur struggled to undo the knots around his hands and feet. It was no good. The ropes were too tight. He clenched his fists. He was trapped. There seemed to be no way out.

How can Arthur escape?

The Plot Thickens

A rthur slid down the rough thatch and landed on the ground with a thud. The camp was quiet. He was free to look for Sleuth and to discover what dirty work Pauncho was up to.

Keeping to the shadows, Arthur crept through the camp. He dodged from cover to cover. There was a noise behind him . . . but it was only someone snoring.

With all senses at red alert, he crept past a lighted window, right under the noses of Pauncho and his side-kick.

Arthur's ears pricked up at what he heard. Pauncho was plotting something sinister. If only Arthur could work out what.

Arthur slumped down feeling very confused and wondered what to do next.

Suddenly, he heard footsteps. He turned, alarmed, to find himself nose to nose with Sleuth.

Sleuth jumped up wagging his tail furiously and dropped the sharp knife he had been carrying.

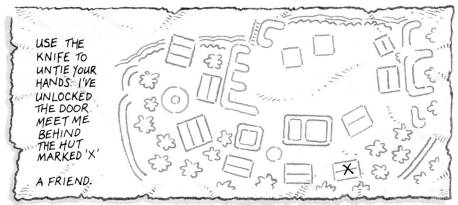

USE THE KNIFE TO UNTIE YOUR HANDS. I'VE UNLOCKED THE DOOR. MEET ME BEHIND THE HUT MARKED 'X'

A FRIEND.

Arthur picked up the knife. There was a piece of paper tied round the handle. On it was a plan of the base and a message. Arthur groaned as he read it. All his great escape work had been unnecessary. But who was this friend in Pauncho's camp?

Arthur studied the map and tried to work out where he was. He thought back to his first view of the base and knew which hut he should go to.

Where is Arthur? Which hut is the one marked X on the map?

Secret Sequence

S leuth led Arthur to where he had hidden their survival kit and, fully prepared, they tiptoed to the meeting place. Suddenly Arthur froze. He spotted a sinister shadow. It was creeping towards them. They were trapped. CLICK . . .

"Nice photo," whispered a cheerful voice. "I'm a friend. My name's Jane Printz."

"The missing photographer," gasped Arthur, handing back the knife. "What are you doing here?"

"I was in the jungle taking photos of the rare Orchid Narcotica," replied Jane, putting the knife in her bag, and handing Arthur a series of photos. "When I came across this base, I realized that something very suspicious was going on."

What was going on? Arthur studied Jane's photos, trying to piece the story together. Suddenly Sleuth growled a warning. They dived for cover as Pauncho and his henchmen marched past towards an old temple covered in vines.

Pauncho pressed four numbered buttons on a panel. Top left, bottom left, Arthur blinked and missed the third, then top right. A heavy steel door opened, the men stepped inside and the door clanged shut.

"Let's follow them," Arthur said. "But what is the sequence that will open the door?"

Can you work out what is going on from the photos? What is the secret sequence?

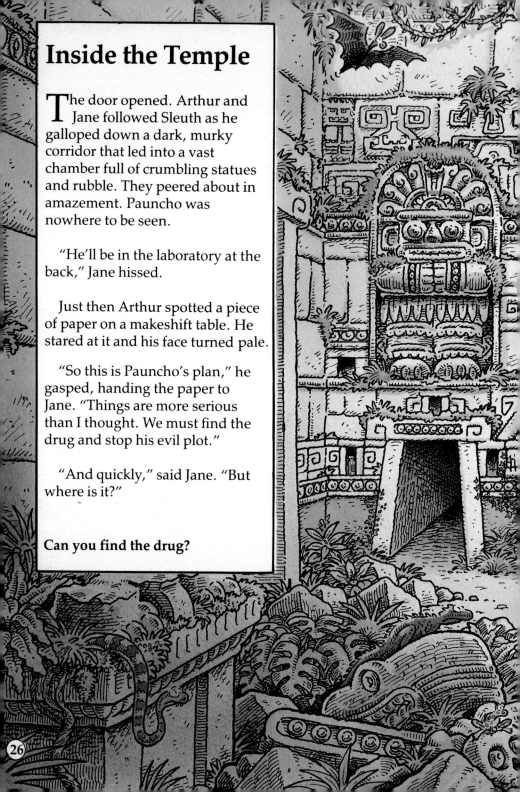

Inside the Temple

The door opened. Arthur and Jane followed Sleuth as he galloped down a dark, murky corridor that led into a vast chamber full of crumbling statues and rubble. They peered about in amazement. Pauncho was nowhere to be seen.

"He'll be in the laboratory at the back," Jane hissed.

Just then Arthur spotted a piece of paper on a makeshift table. He stared at it and his face turned pale.

"So this is Pauncho's plan," he gasped, handing the paper to Jane. "Things are more serious than I thought. We must find the drug and stop his evil plot."

"And quickly," said Jane. "But where is it?"

Can you find the drug?

A Perilous Path

Jane grabbed the drug and gently placed it in her pocket.

"Come on," whispered Arthur. "Let's get out of here, before Pauncho finds us."

Too late! The room echoed with voices, Pauncho was back. Arthur scuttled down a corridor, waving to the others to follow.

Jane tried to stop him, but Arthur had disappeared into the inky blackness. Jane and Sleuth dashed after him at top speed, brushing away sticky cobwebs and dodging sleeping bats.

Suddenly the passage sloped steeply downhill. The trio raced on until they saw light. Arthur sprinted towards it . . .

. . . out onto a sheer rock face. Down below was a fast-flowing river and treacherous ravines. Arthur trod thin air, but Jane caught hold of his arm and pulled him back to safety.

Behind them came Pauncho's angry shouts and the pounding of feet. They were trapped. There was no way back, only down.

Jane desperately looked around. Opposite them was a cliff with a path leading up it. If they reached the top of the cliff, they might be safe. But how could they get there? Jane looked at the maze of paths.

Can you find a safe route to the top of the cliff opposite?

The Rickety Rope Bridge

They scrambled up the steep
path to the top of the cliff.
Jane fumbled for her binoculars.
There was no time to rest. Pauncho
and his men were hot on their trail.

Sleuth raced down the narrow
path on the other side of the cliff.
Arthur and Jane stumbled after
him. Suddenly he started
barking. Ahead was a rickety rope
bridge over a gorge. Crocodiles
were swimming underneath,
jaws snapping. Arthur gulped.

"This is the only way across,"
said Jane, as she and Sleuth
stepped gingerly onto the bridge.
Arthur followed.

The frail rope bridge began to
swing wildly. Jane clung on to the
supports and crawled along.
Arthur trod carefully, trying not
to look down.

"It's not so difficult after all," thought Arthur, halfway across the bridge.

Just then, his foot went through a rotten plank. He tripped and the backpack and machete spiralled down to the crocodiles waiting below. Arthur grabbed a plank and hung on. He hauled himself up inch by painful inch and staggered over to solid ground.

"Safe at last," he gasped.

Bullets whined and ricocheted round him. Jane looked through the binoculars. Pauncho's men were about to cross the bridge.

Arthur knew he had to stop them and started tugging at the pegs. But it was no good – they were dug in too deeply. If only they could cut the ropes.

How can they stop Pauncho's men?

The Next Move

Arthur took charge as he led the trek down into the valley. Progress became slower and slower as the air got hotter and stickier. The steaming vegetation closed in. Every step seemed like a mile through the green foliage.

All of a sudden, there was a deafening thunderclap and raindrops the size of golf balls began to pelt down. Arthur chopped off some leaves to use as umbrellas, while Jane and Sleuth dashed through the jungle, looking for a place to shelter.

They discovered a large hollow tree and scrambled inside. Now to plan the next move.

"Lucky I remembered Rule One of Jungle Journeying," said Arthur, delving into his pockets. "Carry a map and compass at all times."

He triumphantly brandished a map, but the paper was damp and rotten and it fell to pieces.

"We've gone two miles South East from the middle of the rope bridge," he said, trying to fit the pieces of the map together.

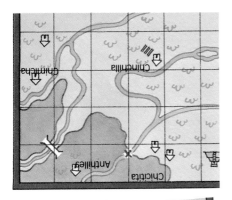

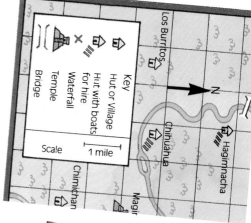

"But where are we heading?" asked Jane.

Arthur looked blank for a second. Then he studied the map and one place name caught his eye. In a flash, he remembered the contact points mentioned in his mission instructions and Agency Memo 521. Today was Wednesday. It was now midday. They had to move fast.

"The quickest way to travel is by river," said Arthur. "But we need a boat."

Together they studied the map and worked out the best route to the nearest Agency contact point.

Where are they?
What is the quickest route to the contact point?

Risky River Crossing

They set off towards the contact point. Arthur checked his compass, Jane read the map and Sleuth barked at swarms of biting insects. They dragged themselves through a muddy mess of rotting leaves as water splashed down from the trees.

On they squelched through sticky black mud until they stopped at the river bank. Where was the bridge? Arthur stared around in horror. It had been washed away by the flooded river. Only a few shattered remains were left.

"It's stopped raining at least," said Jane, peering out from under her leaf. "Let's wait for the water to subside, then we can cross."

"It will take too long," said Arthur, looking at the swollen torrent rushing past.

"We must cross the river to get to the fishing hut," he continued. "If we put our heads together, we're bound to come up with a plan."

Can you find a safe route across the river using Jane's and Arthur's ideas?

Raft Craft

Jane checked that the drug was still safe in her pocket as Sleuth led her and Arthur to a deserted shack made from planks and barrels.

They hunted around for a boat to sail downstream but all they could find was a sunken wreck. Arthur wracked his brains. The only thing to do was to make a raft. But how? He had missed Survival Lesson R for Raft Building and Repairs.

Time was running out for them. Suddenly Sleuth started tugging at Arthur's pocket. There was a ripping noise followed by a dull thud as a heavy book fell to the ground.

"Well done Sleuth," shouted Arthur, grabbing the book and flicking through the pages. "I'd forgotten about this. It's my copy of the Action Agency Survive and Succeed Handbook. It's got raft designs in it."

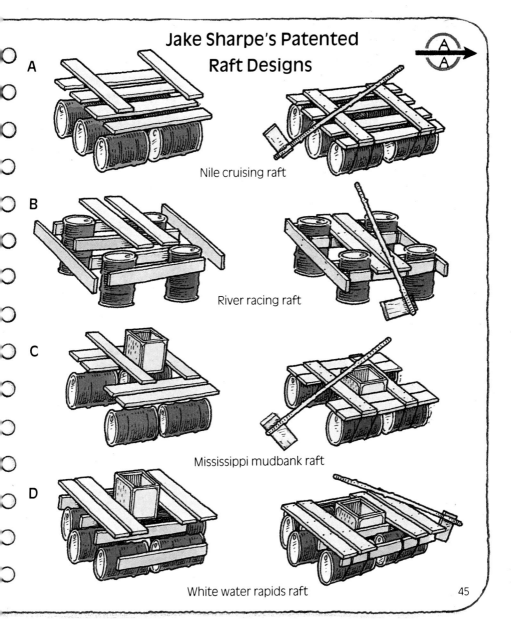

Jake Sharpe's Patented Raft Designs

Nile cruising raft

River racing raft

Mississippi mudbank raft

White water rapids raft

45

Jane scouted around for raft building materials, while Sleuth sniffed out a hammer, a long coil of rope and some rusty nails. Arthur puzzled over the designs then he checked the equipment that Jane and Sleuth had found.

"It's no good after all," he sighed. "All but four barrels leak and three of the planks are rotten. We can't build a raft."

Is Arthur right?
Can they build a raft?

River Journey

A rthur lashed the final plank into position. Jane prodded the raft gingerly, as Sleuth suspiciously stepped aboard.

"Let's go," shouted Arthur, carrying two bamboo poles. "We're running out of time."

He pushed them clear of the bank, but not clear of trouble. A strong current swept the raft downstream, round mudbanks and through the treacherous waters. Arthur battled to keep them afloat, while Jane and Sleuth fought off the dangers that lay round every corner.

The current began to slacken off. The raft floated on between a triangular island and a small thin island. Suddenly a loud roaring noise filled the air. Waterfalls dead ahead!

"We've got two choices," Arthur said, remembering his Action Agency River Training Course. "We can send the raft downstream and trek overland to meet it. Or we could dismantle the raft and carry it past the falls."

"Neither," said Jane, studying the map. "I know what to do."

What should they do and why?

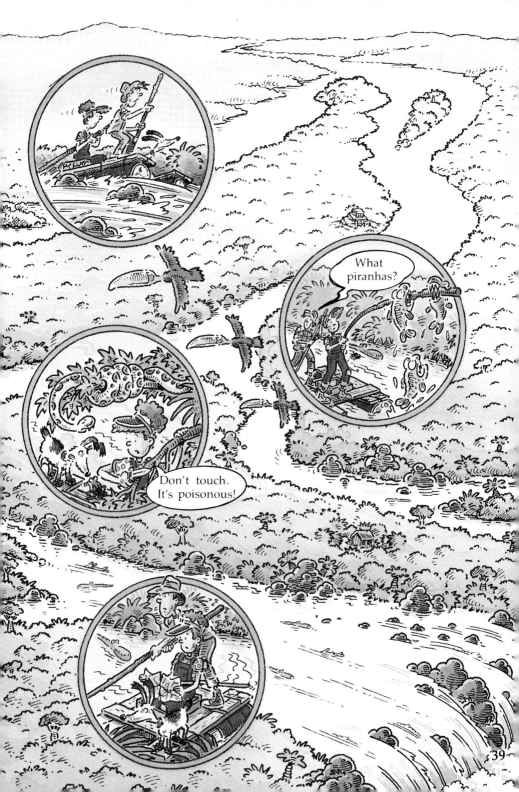

39

The Meeting

The raft jolted and bumped hard against the river bank throwing Arthur, Jane and Sleuth ashore. They landed in a confused heap.

As they untangled the mess of arms and legs, Jane caught sight of a thatched shack in the middle of a clearing . . . This was the contact point.

"Be careful," whispered Arthur. "We don't know who might be in there."

They tiptoed silently into the clearing, on the look-out for signs of life. Sleuth's nose began to twitch. He growled quietly and scampered towards the hut. Jane and Arthur followed hard on his heels. They peered through a window and gasped in horror.

Inside the hut was . . . Pauncho! Sitting opposite him, at the other end of a long table was a mysterious, crooked looking stranger surrounded by piles of used money.

"We've been set-up," gasped Jane. "The journey was a wild goose chase. We've walked straight into Pauncho's trap."

But Arthur wasn't so sure. His memory flashed back to the conversation he overheard in Pauncho's camp and he scanned the room. Arthur spotted two things that were rather odd.

"Maybe not," he said.

What has Arthur spotted?

The Mysterious Stranger

Arthur sprang into action. With lightning speed, he vaulted through the window, disarmed Pauncho and tied him up.

Then Arthur spun round to confront the stranger and came face to face with . . .

"Uncle Jake!" gasped Arthur. "What are you doing here?"

"Congratulations Arthur and friends," boomed a deep voice. "You've just tied up the loose ends of Operation Orchid."

"A section of the Action Agency Jungle Squad have already cleaned up Pauncho's camp," explained Uncle Jake, "And Pauncho's given us the drug."

"It's a fake," said Arthur, "Jane's got the real stuff."

But Jane's pockets were empty. Where was the drug? Suddenly Sleuth barked.

"Don't worry," smiled Arthur. "We'll find it. Follow that dog."

Where is the drug?

Clues

You will need to hold this page in front of a mirror to read the clues.

Pages 4-5

Look at the Action Code on the pinboard on page 3. A = ∞ B = Δ

Pages 6-7

First find the gap in the fence. The rest is easy. They can use boxes, crates and sacks as cover, and the music should drown most of the noise they make creeping through the base.

Pages 10-11

Try swapping the first and last letters of each word.

Pages 12-13

The pictures show the view looking due North, South, East and West. Which is which? Try matching the landmarks in the pictures with the landmarks on the map.

Pages 14-15

This is easy. Use your eyes.

Pages 16-17

You don't need a clue for this. Look out for trail signs.

Pages 18-19

Look at the Crookfax papers on page 5.

Pages 20-21

Look at all the things in the hut. What can he use to help him escape?

Pages 22-23

Turn the map the other way up and look at the picture of the base on pages 18-19.

Pages 24-25

The numbers form a sequence, or pattern. The gap between the numbers increases by 1 each time.

Pages 26-27

What does the drug look like? Check the conversation on page 22 and the photo on page 25.

Pages 28-29

This is easy. They can crawl across tree trunks.

Pages 30-31

What was Jane's message attached to? Look back to page 23.

Pages 32-33

This is tricky. Trace or photocopy the map pieces and fit them together. The pictures on pages 28-31 should help you locate the rope bridge on the map. The scale of the map is shown in the key. Look at Arthur's mission instructions on page 5 and Memo 521 on page 3. An anagram is a word made by arranging the letters in a different order.

Pages 34-35

Study each idea in turn. Which ones will work and which will not?

Pages 36-37

How many barrels and planks can they use?

Pages 38-39

Compare the picture with the map on page 33.

Pages 40-41

What was Pauncho saying on page 22? Use your eyes.

Page 42

Did Jane drop the bottle somewhere on the journey?

Answers

Pages 4-5

The message is written in Action Code. This is what it says:

MISSION INSTRUCTIONS FOR ACTION AGENT 770. INVESTIGATE CONTENTS OF PLANE AT OLD AIRFIELD. REPORT TO CONTACT POINTS AT QH, DONNOL, WONKYER OR HAGIMNACHIC BY WEDNESDAY 1600 HOURS.

Pages 6-7

The safe route is marked in black.

They crawl behind the sacks and the hut.

Pages 10-11

The message is decoded by swapping the first and last letters of each word. This is what it says:

MIND CONTROL PLAN A. VITAL EQUIPMENT AND SUPPLIES READY FOR TRANSPORTATION ON MONDAY FROM THE OLD AIRFIELD. AIM FOR LANDING STRIP AT E1, THEN

PROCEED TO BASE AT H1 VIA MARKED TRAIL. FILE FALSE FLIGHT PLAN. IN CASE OF EMERGENCY, BAIL OUT AND CONTACT BASE. NO RESCUE ATTEMPTS WILL BE MADE. THESE ORDERS ARE ISSUED BY THE BOSS AND MUST BE OBEYED AT ALL COSTS.

Pages 12-13

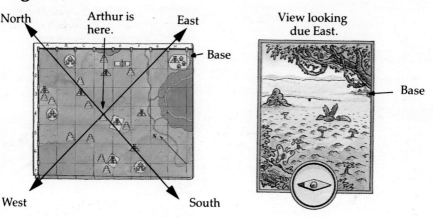

North — Arthur is here. — East — Base

West — South

View looking due East. — Base

Pages 14-15

Arthur has spotted a cross painted on a tree trunk. Sleuth has spotted a snake.

Snake

Cross

Pages 16-17

The trail is marked in black.

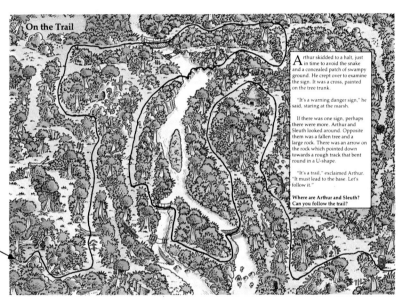

On the Trail

Arthur skidded to a halt, just in time to avoid the snake and a concealed patch of swampy ground. He crept over to examine the sign. It was a cross, painted on the tree trunk.

"It's a warning danger sign," he said, staring at the marsh.

If there was one sign, perhaps there were more. Arthur and Sleuth looked around. Opposite them was a fallen tree and a large rock. There was an arrow on the rock which pointed down towards a rough track that bent round in a U-shape.

"It's a trail," exclaimed Arthur. "It must lead to the base. Let's follow it."

Where are Arthur and Sleuth? Can you follow the trail?

Sleuth and Arthur are here.

Pages 18-19

Arthur recognizes this man, El Pauncho, from the Action Agency Crookfax on page 5.

45

Pages 20-21

There are several possible ways to escape, but this is the easiest.

1. Arthur cuts the ropes round his hands with the broken bottle and unties the ropes around his feet.

3. Next he pulls himself up onto the beams and climbs up and out through the hole in the roof.

2. Then he moves a crate to the centre of the hut and climbs onto it.

4. He slides down the thatched roof and jumps to the ground.

Pages 22-23

Arthur is here.

This is the hut marked X on the map.

USE THE KNIFE TO UNTIE YOUR HANDS. I'VE UNLOCKED THE DOOR MEET ME BEHIND THE HUT MARKED 'X'

A FRIEND.

Pages 24-25

The photos tell a story:

A plane lands in the jungle. El Pauncho and his men step out. Pauncho issues orders which clearly relate to the formula for a powerful mind control drug, made from the extract of the Orchid Narcotica plant. The plants are harvested in the jungle, loaded into baskets and taken to an old temple. Here, one of Pauncho's cronies carries out the distillation process to produce the drug. Then Sleuth and Arthur appear on the scene. Arthur is taken prisoner and Sleuth sets off to rescue him with a message from Jane, wrapped around a knife.

To open the temple door, they need to press the buttons 2, 3, 5 and 8. These numbers form a sequence, or pattern, with the gap between the numbers increasing by 1 each time.

Pages 26-27

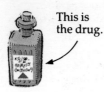

This is the drug.

It is hidden here.

Pages 28-29

The safe route is marked in black.

Use the rocks as stepping stones to cross the water.

Move the tree trunk and use it to bridge the ravine.

Pages 30-31

They can cut the ropes securing the bridge with Jane's knife – the one she gave to Sleuth with the message for Arthur (page 23). When Arthur gave the knife back to Jane (page 24), she put it into her bag.

Pages 32-33

The quickest route is marked in black.

They are here.

CHIMICHANGA, the contact point.

This is how Arthur worked it all out:

1. He located the rope bridge on the map by thinking back to the landscape nearby (pages 28-31).

2. Then he drew a line twice the length of the one shown in the key running South East from the centre of the bridge.

3. Next he remembered his mission instructions (page 5) which mentioned four possible contact points (QH, DONNOL, WONKYER AND HAGIMNACHIC).

4. Then he remembered the Action Agency Memo 521 (page 3). This is written in Action Code and it says: FROM NOW ON UNTIL FURTHER NOTICE ALL AGENCY CONTACT POINTS WILL BE WRITTEN AS ANAGRAMS.

5. Arthur knew that an anagram is a word made by arranging the letters in a different order and worked out that HAGIMNACHIC is an anagram of CHIMICHANGA.

6. The rest was easy. The quickest route to Chimichanga is by river via the hut with boats for hire marked HAGIMNACHA.

47

Pages 34-35

Stepping on a crocodile isn't wise.

This is possible but risky. It's easy to lose balance.

The plank is cracked and rotten.

The gap is too wide to jump across.

Pages 36-37

They can build the Mississippi mudbank raft.

Pages 38-39

They have passed the tributary leading to the contact point. They must head for the bank and get off the raft. They can walk along the bank pulling the raft and cross the tributary on the raft. The contact point is a short walk into the jungle.

Pages 40-41

The crooked looking stranger sitting opposite Pauncho has FOUR fingers on each hand, yet Pauncho was planning to meet the man with THREE fingers (page 22). The Action Agency logo is clearly visible on a piece of paper in the man's briefcase.

Page 42

The bottle dropped out of Jane's pocket as they came ashore.

AGENT ARTHUR
ON THE
STORMY SEAS

Martin Oliver

Illustrated by

Paddy Mounter

Designed by
David Gillingwater

Additional designs by Sarah Dixon

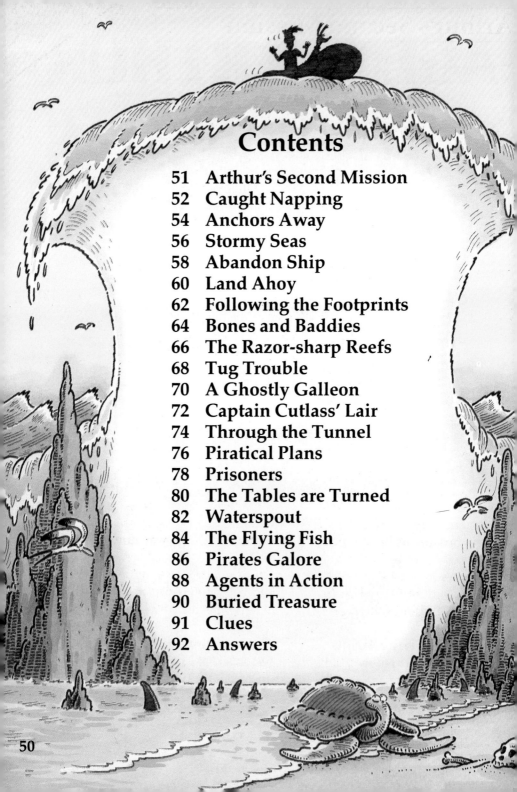

Contents

Arthur's Second Mission

Following the success of his first mission, Arthur was smiling broadly as he stepped out of the jungle and into the busy streets of Port Pacamac. He had been sent there by Uncle Jake, the founder of the Agency.

"This looks like a relaxing place," Arthur whispered to his faithful companion, Sleuth. "No signs of our arch enemies The Spider Organization. We've seen the last of them I'm sure."

Dodging past local sea captains and ducking flying missiles, Arthur made his way down to the harbour. He stared hard at the vital Agency information that he had been given and tried to keep his eyes peeled and ears open.

"Remember, an Action Agent should always be on the alert," he said to Sleuth. "You never know when we might have to put our finely-tuned skills into action."

Caught Napping

Arthur sat down in a crumbling quayside cafe. He ordered his favourite tutti-frutti cocktail and gazed out over Pacamac Bay. Despite what he had heard about ships disappearing, everything seemed normal.

"Uncle Jake must have thought we deserved a holiday," he said to Sleuth, who opened one eye then fell asleep again.

Arthur leant back and closed his eyes. He dreamt he was on a beach and all was quiet except for footsteps approaching then retreating into the distance.

Arthur woke up with a start, blinking in the sunlight. He looked down at the table. His drink had arrived – along with a grubby envelope. Sleuth snored quietly on while Arthur glanced around. There was no sign of the silent messenger.

Arthur ripped open the envelope. Inside he found a piece of paper covered with instantly recognizable symbols. It was a message from the Action Agency.

What does the message say?

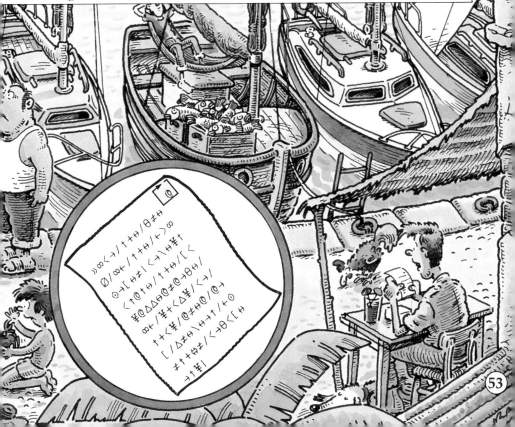

Anchors Away

Arthur spotted The Flounder, a three-masted schooner moored at the far side of the port. He dashed over to it. The captain smiled and took Arthur on as a deckhand. Introductions were hardly over before the captain boomed out orders to weigh anchor and cast off.

"We'll keep a low profile," whispered Arthur, as they set sail into the wide blue yonder. "And act like old sea-dogs."

But Arthur's stomach had different ideas. While Sleuth scampered round happily, Arthur struggled to find his sea-legs.

Arthur eventually got used to the motion of the ship, but there was hardly time to rest as the captain ordered "All hands on deck to learn ship safety."

"So much for a holiday," said Arthur, trying to concentrate on the ship's emergency drill.

For the first week The Flounder made good progress, sailing at full speed with a stiff breeze behind her.

Arthur learnt to steer as Captain Tar plotted their course through squalls, showers and schools of dolphins.

During the second week at sea, Kate spotted a dot on the horizon and shouted "Land Ahoy."

The crew anchored the boat and stepped onto a jetty. While Captain Tar traded some of their cargo, the others tried to get back their land-legs.

The following night Captain Tar gathered the crew together and told them a strange story.

"Ships disappear mysteriously in these waters," he said. "Some say the ghost ship of pirate Captain Cutlass still sails the seas, looking for victims."

On the third day's sail from the island, the wind died away. The sea became dead calm and the sails hung limply.

Arthur, Jim and Kate could only doze and dream as the air became hot and heavy. But Captain Tar didn't seem to mind.

They were still becalmed next morning when Arthur's night watch finished. Arthur was about to turn in when he saw Captain Tar tap the barometer uneasily.

"I hope those clouds don't mean trouble," yawned Arthur, as he headed below decks.

Stormy Seas

Arthur and Sleuth snoozed fitfully while the wind howled and waves broke against the porthole.

The Flounder sailed on as flashes of lightning streaked down from the dark clouds onto the sea.

Suddenly the ship listed over to port. Arthur and Sleuth flew out of their bunk and hit the deck.

Arthur picked himself up and desperately scrambled into his waterproofs. He and Jim dashed out of the cabin.

Up on deck, Kate and the captain were struggling with the wheel, trying to turn the ship to face the next wave.

But it was too late. An enormous wave raced towards The Flounder.

It towered high above the ship for a second, then broke over the prow.

Tons of salty water streamed across the deck, slamming into the crew.

Abandon ship.

The Flounder rolled and dipped under the weight of water, then slowly rose.

The main mast had snapped like a twig and the sails were in tatters.

Captain Tar roared orders above the gale, as the crew clung on for dear life.

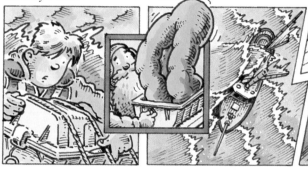

Jim cut through the lashings holding the life raft. Captain Tar pulled a ripcord to inflate it.

More waves crashed broadside into the stricken ship as Kate and Arthur scrambled below deck.

Water was pouring into the cabin as Kate grabbed vital equipment. Arthur tried the radio.

It was dead. Arthur yanked open a drawer in the captain's desk and grabbed the logbook, a map and a note. Arthur noticed something strange.

The note was in code. But he only had time to glance at it, before stuffing it into a pocket.

What does it say?

Abandon Ship

Arthur struggled out of the cabin and joined the others up on deck. He clung onto the guardrail as the ship rolled and pitched unsteadily. The life raft was already floating on the churning sea.

Kate got ready to join Jim aboard the raft. Clutching her equipment bag tightly, she leapt over the side.

Arthur gulped, it was his turn now. He picked up Sleuth and looked over. The raft bounced up and down in the heavy swell, banging against The Flounder's hull then drifting away.

"It's all in the timing," thought Arthur, just as a gust of wind blew him off the ship . . . and into the inflatable.

Kate untangled herself from the others and stared at The Flounder. Something was wrong.

"The mooring rope's snapped," she gasped.

As they helplessly watched the captain drift away, Jim realized the raft was taking in water. They had to bail it out, and fast.

Five hours later the hurricane had blown itself out and the raft was floating in calm sea. Arthur opened the door flap and stared around. There was water, water everywhere, but no sign of The Flounder or of Captain Tar.

Sleuth growled at a shark and Arthur's mind raced back to his Shipwreck Survival Course.

They must try to pinpoint their position to see if they were near land. Jim checked the compass while Arthur studied The Flounder's logbook. Kate noticed they were drifting in a current. Arthur thought hard and picked up the chart. Now he could work out where they were.

Where are they?

Land Ahoy

During the damp and cramped night, Arthur decided to tell the twins about the Action Agency and to enlist their help on his mission. They listened in amazement and eagerly agreed to become Apprentice Action Agents. As dawn broke Arthur spotted low clouds on the horizon.

Just then a seabird landed by the raft. Sleuth licked his lips hopefully, while Arthur's brain whirred and clicked. Could these signs mean land ahead? Jim and Kate whooped happily at the thought and began paddling.

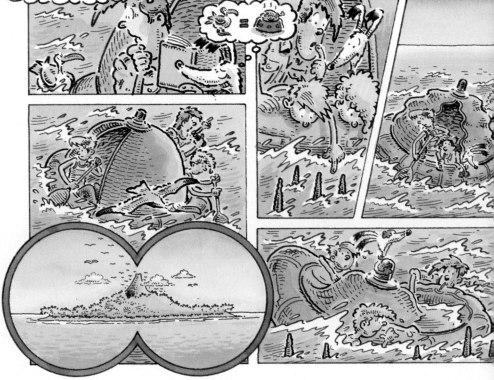

Arthur picked up his all-weather, extra-tough, mega-magnifying Action Agency issue binoculars and scanned the horizon. A coral island zoomed into focus.

"Land ahoy," he shouted.

Kate and Jim went into overpaddle. The raft raced along until Kate heard a rip, then a hissing sound. They were punctured! Arthur blew into the flotation chamber while the others tried to steer towards the island, avoiding more coral.

But it was no good. Despite all their efforts, they were still deflating fast.

"Abandon ship," panted Arthur.

They floated out of the raft and half-swimming, half-wading, dragged themselves ashore.

"Safe at last," gasped Jack, collapsing on the beach. "We're alone on a deserted island."

"Maybe we're not," said Kate.

What has Kate spotted?

Following the Footprints

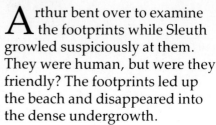

Hmm, size 12 man's.

Arthur bent over to examine the footprints while Sleuth growled suspiciously at them. They were human, but were they friendly? The footprints led up the beach and disappeared into the dense undergrowth.

"Let's follow them," said Jim. "They may lead to civilization."

"Sleuth can sniff the way," Arthur replied. "We'll follow, but stay alert."

A parrot screeched overhead as the trio tramped uphill behind Sleuth, their mouths watering at the delicious-looking tropical fruits all around.

A few minutes later Sleuth barked angrily. The trail ended abruptly at a pool of water and a waterfall. Kate rested her sore feet while Jim wondered what they should do next.

Arthur looked up. Whoever had made the trail of footprints must have swum across the pool and climbed the cliff opposite.

After telling the twins to carry on searching, Arthur waded through the shallow water at the edge of the pool and began scrambling up the rocks. Trying not to look down, he gradually left Jim and Kate far behind.

It was a long hot climb, but at last Arthur reached the top. Once he had got his breath back, he wiped the sweat from his eyes and scanned the island hoping to see some trace of civilization or even of Captain Tar.

But there was no sign of human life, only a seabird that flapped its wings and gazed curiously back at him. Arthur slumped down dejectedly beside Sleuth. He wondered what they should do next. They didn't want to be stuck on a desert island.

Back at the pool Kate explored the waterfall but found nothing. She was swimming back, when Jim spotted a scrap of paper. He picked it up and realized it was written in code.

"I think it describes a trail," he shouted. "If we follow it we might find help."

"Or pirate treasure," Kate added hopefully. "But where can we pick it up?"

Where can they join the trail?

63

Bones and Baddies

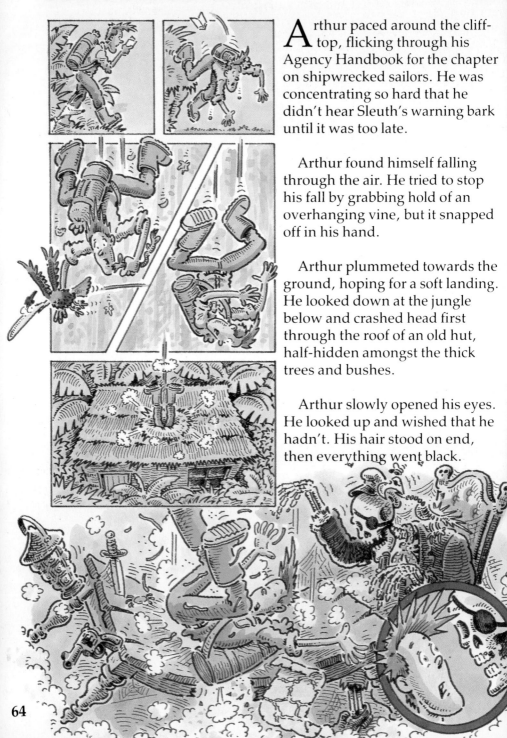

Arthur paced around the clifftop, flicking through his Agency Handbook for the chapter on shipwrecked sailors. He was concentrating so hard that he didn't hear Sleuth's warning bark until it was too late.

Arthur found himself falling through the air. He tried to stop his fall by grabbing hold of an overhanging vine, but it snapped off in his hand.

Arthur plummeted towards the ground, hoping for a soft landing. He looked down at the jungle below and crashed head first through the roof of an old hut, half-hidden amongst the thick trees and bushes.

Arthur slowly opened his eyes. He looked up and wished that he hadn't. His hair stood on end, then everything went black.

Meanwhile Kate and Jim were following the trail. Jim spotted two people ahead. He was about to rush up to them when Kate stopped him.

"I don't like the sound of what they're saying," she whispered. "Let's stay hidden."

Jim nodded and stepped back . . . onto a dry twig. It cracked loudly. Kate and Jim froze in horror then turned to run.

But it was too late. Before they could escape, they felt hands on their shoulders and unfriendly faces stared at them.

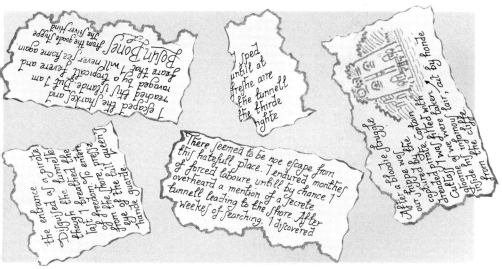

At that moment Sleuth licked Arthur back to consciousness. Arthur was about to race out of the hut when the remains of an old document caught his eye. He began fitting the bits together and working out the writing.

"What a find," thought Arthur, carefully tucking the pieces into his bulging bag. "I must show this to Jim and Kate."

What does the document say?

The Razor-sharp Reefs

A rthur was heading back towards the waterfall when Sleuth sniffed the air and growled. Arthur glimpsed movement on the beach. He looked closer and gasped. Jim and Kate were being pushed into a rowing boat.

Arthur raced down through the trees and thick bushes to the beach. He stared across the lagoon. The twins were being taken towards a rusty old tug boat. Sleuth sniffed at a scrap of blue paper and gave it to Arthur.

"This is no time to pick up litter," hissed Arthur, putting it in his pocket. "We must find a way through the razor-sharp coral to that tug."

Can Arthur find a safe route to the boat?

Tug Trouble

Arthur trod water and oil as he tried to fathom out a way aboard the old tug. He heaved himself out of the water to reach a porthole in the side of the ship. But he couldn't make it.

Then Arthur had a flash of inspiration and swam over to the slimy anchor chain. He hoisted himself up link by slippery link, until at last he clambered over the side of the ship.

He landed on the deck and hid behind a battered funnel. He peered out and saw the twins being led below decks by two mean-looking villains. Who were these crooks? Why had they kidnapped Jim and Kate?

Arthur turned to Sleuth, but he wasn't there. Arthur looked back over the side and spotted a dorsal fin. He threw Sleuth a line and hauled him up, just in time. Sleuth collapsed in a damp puddle and the tug set sail.

Hours later the boat was echoing to the sound of snoring as the stowaways crept out from behind the funnel. Arthur stared inside the wheelhouse, trying to find Jim and Kate. Then he tiptoed below decks to check out the crew's quarters.

Arthur followed his nose and peered in at the galley. He left quickly. Sleuth led the way down to another deck and growled outside a steel door. Kate and Jim were in the cabin ahead. They seemed to be all right but they were well guarded.

You should always lock the engine room door and leave the key in the lock.

Just then Arthur heard footsteps coming their way. He stared round in horror then dived through an open door into the engine room. Arthur hid behind the steamy old engine and strained to hear the muffled conversation outside.

His heart sank as he heard the key click in the lock. He was trapped! Arthur looked round the grimy room and spurred himself into action. There must be a way out, and he was going to find it.

Is there a way out?

A Ghostly Galleon

It was dark when Arthur managed to open the door and he crept silently above decks. The ship was moored in a lagoon. The moon was shining and mist rose off the sea. In the distance Arthur spotted Jim and Kate being rowed towards an island.

Just then Sleuth's hackles rose as a faint chugging noise drifted over the water. Suddenly an old sailing ship appeared through the mist. Arthur stared wide-eyed at the tattered sails, the skull and cross bones and the ghostly crew.

"H . . h . . help," he quavered, his hair standing on end.

Arthur remembered Captain Tar's story and turned white. His Agency Training hadn't covered spooky spectres, and this looked very much like the ghostly galleon of pirate Captain Cutlass.

Is it?

Captain Cutlass' Lair

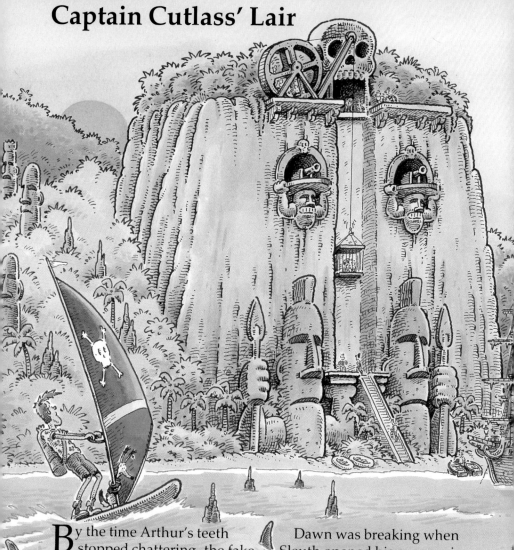

By the time Arthur's teeth stopped chattering, the fake ghosts had changed course for the island that the twins had been taken to. Were the kidnappers in league with the creepy crew? There was only one possible way to find out.

"We'll follow them," Arthur said, lowering a sail board into the water. "Hang on Sleuth."

Dawn was breaking when Sleuth opened his eyes again. Arthur windsurfed unsteadily round a headland and gasped.

He spotted the twins. They were inside a cage being winched up a fortress-like cliff. Arthur stared in amazement and thought back to the memoirs of Bosun Bones. This was the entrance to Captain Cutlass' pirate lair.

Arthur swung the sail round, regained his balance and headed for dry land. At last he beached the board out of sight of the villains. Sleuth bounded happily onto solid ground and scampered round the huge stone heads that were scattered along the shore.

"I must try to rescue Jim and Kate and find out what these crooks are up to," Arthur thought. "But the front entrance is impregnable. If only there's a back way in."

Arthur began scrambling up the steep hill for a better view of the base. Suddenly he tripped over the overgrown head of a fallen statue.

As he picked himself up, his memory jolted into gear and he reached for Bosun Bones' memoirs. Maybe there was a way into the base after all?

How can Arthur get in?

Through the Tunnel

A rthur climbed the head and pressed the eye. There was a grinding sound below and a stone slab slid open. Arthur shone his torch into the blackness and the air was full of dark flying shapes.

Arthur fought off the bats and he and Sleuth headed into the tunnel. Water dripped from the ceiling and their footsteps echoed off the stone walls as they crept slowly uphill.

Sleuth was first out of the tunnel and into the cave. He sniffed the air then listened out by the door. Arthur picked up some photos on a desk. He stared hard at them. His brain whirred as he spotted the two kidnappers, the fake ghost ship and its crew.

Arthur immediately recognized the names of the boats in the photos. That solved the mystery of the missing ships. Arthur smiled grimly. The first part of his mission was complete; now to find out more about these modern-day pirates.

Suddenly Arthur stopped. Ahead he spotted light at the end of the tunnel. Arthur and Sleuth cautiously scrambled over fallen stones, peered through the hole and gasped.

The cave in front of them was crammed full of radar screens and hi-tech tracking equipment. But there was no trace of Kate and Jim or any other sign of life. What was going on?

```
to organization spider and mangler
max lil patch eye the have we the
for route ship target next fish
flying the sail will it the between
sw and graveyard ships island
peaks twin the reaching until the
of northernmost here needles three
turn will it nw head and with level
until in island easternmost then
archipelago diamond cruise will it
between s due and island shark then
and volcano our of out an if
territory use occurs emergency jpx
plan escape
```

Who was behind the villains, and what was their next target? Just then a printer chattered into life. Arthur hardly had time to memorize the coded type before Sleuth growled. Seconds later the door opened and a familiar figure walked in.

Arthur peered at the pirate. If she was here, the twins must be nearby. But before Arthur started searching for them, he tried to decode the message. It might answer some questions.

What does the message say?

75

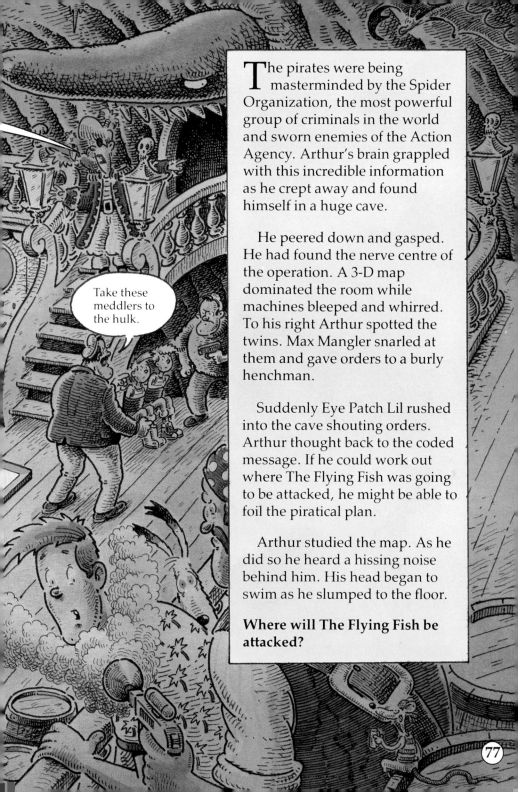

Take these meddlers to the hulk.

The pirates were being masterminded by the Spider Organization, the most powerful group of criminals in the world and sworn enemies of the Action Agency. Arthur's brain grappled with this incredible information as he crept away and found himself in a huge cave.

He peered down and gasped. He had found the nerve centre of the operation. A 3-D map dominated the room while machines bleeped and whirred. To his right Arthur spotted the twins. Max Mangler snarled at them and gave orders to a burly henchman.

Suddenly Eye Patch Lil rushed into the cave shouting orders. Arthur thought back to the coded message. If he could work out where The Flying Fish was going to be attacked, he might be able to foil the piratical plan.

Arthur studied the map. As he did so he heard a hissing noise behind him. His head began to swim as he slumped to the floor.

Where will The Flying Fish be attacked?

Prisoners

Take him to the hulk.

Run Sleuth.

He's coming round.

Arthur's mind groggily drifted in and out of consciousness. As he tried to fight his way out of the drug-induced sleep, images of what had happened filtered through to him.

He dimly remembered faces and being moved out of the cave, but who were the strange people looking down at him, and where was he now?

We're aboard the prison ship and we can't move unless we untie these ropes.

Arthur blinked again at the two blurs staring at him. Kate and Jim suddenly appeared.

They explained the situation and Arthur's mind snapped back into action. He heard a strange noise coming from the porthole.

"Good work," whispered Arthur, as a bedraggled Sleuth squeezed into the cabin. "Bite through our ropes and we'll try and find a way up on deck. From there we might be able to escape."

How can they get up on deck?

The Tables are Turned

Arthur was first up on deck. He hid behind the capstan as the twins scrambled out of the hatch behind him.

"We must keep quiet until the coast is clear," whispered Arthur. "Once the pirates have gone below we will try to take a boat and reach The Flying Fish before it's attacked."

They heard laughter from the deck below and peered round the mast. Kate clenched her fists at what she saw.

"Those are the crews of the captured ships," she said. "We can't leave them as prisoners."

Kate was right, but there were only three of them against the pirates. Arthur gritted his teeth. He was an Action Agent. There was only one thing to do.

"Charge," yelled Arthur, grabbing a rope and swinging into a crowd of pirates. The twins followed up with a barrel.

The pirates were so surprised that they hardly had time to react before the captured crews joined in on Arthur's side. They soon turned the tables on the dastardly pirate crew.

The Turn Turtle's top speed is 25 knots an hour. But she's low on fuel. Her capacity's 320 nautical miles, but the tank is only a quarter full.

The Rust Bucket can do 20 knots an hour, but her engine's damaged. You must stop every hour and let her cool for 25 minutes.

The Barnacle as rammed by the tes. Any more than 12 knots an hour and she'll sink.

The Sea Spray's engine can reach 12 knots an hour. But with a good wind like today and full sail, she can do a quarter as much again.

As the villains were taken below, Arthur looked back at the island. No one had raised the alarm. Arthur began to grin but it faded when he checked the time. They only had six hours to reach The Flying Fish before the pirates, and it was 90 nautical miles away.

Arthur realized that if they all tried to escape, the pirates in the base would notice. At last the captain of one of the captured ships stepped forwards.

"We can take care of ourselves here if there's any trouble," he said. "You go with the twins and take any one of our boats that's in a seaworthy state."

Arthur listened to what the sailors were saying. There didn't seem to be one boat that would get them to The Flying Fish in time, or was there?

Which boat can they take?

Waterspout

J im and Kate helped Arthur
aboard The Sea Spray. Kate
went below to start the engine
and the motley crew sprang into
action. Arthur pulled out his
Agency compass and grabbed the
rudder. Jim pumped out the
bilges, while Sleuth tried to hoist
the sails.

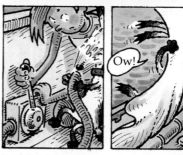

Wishing that Captain Tar was
there to help, Arthur steered a
course through the choppy water.
Kate left the engine and acted as
lookout. They made good
headway despite heavy seas.

After five hours rolling and
pitching, Kate spotted something
on the horizon.

"Look out," she yelled. "It's a
waterspout."

Arthur's blood froze as the
column of water raced towards
them. There was no escape.
Gale force winds blasted around
them and they were sucked into
the whirling waterspout.

Arthur felt himself being lifted up, spun round and round, then hurled deep into the water. His head was spinning and his lungs were bursting as he swam up to the surface. At last his head broke through the water and he gulped down fresh air. Still gasping for breath, he tried to think. Even his Action Agency Training hadn't covered this situation.

Arthur spotted Sleuth floating amongst the remains of the boat. As Sleuth clung onto Arthur's equipment bag, Jim and Kate swam over towards them. Arthur saw a large piece of wreckage floating nearby and spluttered out orders to the others.

"We're in a bad way," Arthur muttered, clambering onto the makeshift raft. "No food, no water, no sign of help."

Just then Kate shouted "Ship ahoy!" and pointed to a dot on the horizon. The crew jumped up and down waving. But it was no good. The ship kept going.

Arthur emptied out his bag and thought back to Captain Tar's emergency signals. If only he could remember the correct signals and find something to signal with.

What can they use to signal?
What signals should they use?

Get aboard the wreckage. We'll use it as a raft.

83

The Flying Fish

As the gleaming boat lowered rescue nets and powered towards the raft, Kate pointed to the name painted on its bows. Arthur gasped. It was The Flying Fish. They began climbing up and Arthur glanced at his watch, there was no time to lose.

At last Arthur pulled himself up and over the guard rail. As soon as his feet touched the deck, he looked round for the captain then raced towards him. The captain backed away, looking worried as Arthur began telling him about the pirates.

The captain listened kindly, then led Arthur and the twins out of the sun. He took them below decks, past cameras and thick steel doors.

Why was there so much security? Kate asked the captain who unlocked a door and showed them into a room . . .

It was packed full of gold, jewels and treasure. Arthur and the twins gasped.

"These art treasures belong to world-famous museums. We are shipping them to . . ." the captain began when he was suddenly interrupted by a shout from above: "Raft ahoy."

The Action Agents were hard on the heels of the captain as he raced up to the bridge, picked up his telescope and trained it on a floating speck.

"More shipwreck victims," the captain muttered. "Probably hit by the waterspout. Stop engines. Stand by to pick them up."

Arthur peered through the telescope and stared closely at the shipwrecked sailors on the raft. Suddenly he noticed that some things were very wrong.

"Don't stop," he yelled frantically. "It's a trap."

What has Arthur noticed?

Pirates Galore

In the nick of time, the captain ordered "Full steam ahead" and swerved his ship past the fake survivors.

"Hooray," shouted Kate, but she was cut short by Sleuth's warning bark.

The sea frothed and churned as a submarine surfaced beside the furious pirates. They abandoned their swamped raft and scrambled aboard the menacing craft.

"Torpedo," screamed Jim. "Coming straight for us."

As they raced for the islands Arthur ran into the bridge and frantically tried to radio for help. But it was no good, his messages were being jammed. Then Sleuth growled angrily. Arthur looked up and gasped in horror.

The pirate ship was right beside them. Arthur spotted Eye Patch Lil snarling as she prepared to fire the cannons.

"All hands on deck," yelled Kate. "Stand by to repel boarders."

The captain flicked the engine to full throttle, but the torpedo was still on a collision course. Jim braced himself for the inevitable explosion just as the ship accelerated and lifted itself out of the water. The torpedo passed harmlessly underneath.

Jim opened his eyes in amazement. They were aboard a hydrofoil. The captain took evasive action and set a course for the shallow water and safety of the Roba Roba islands. Kate shouted warnings as they zigzagged to avoid torpedoes.

Arthur reached the prow. He saw the Roba Roba Islands ahead and more ships speeding in from starboard. They were trapped! Arthur recognized a figure on one of the boats. It was Captain Tar – so he was a pirate too!

Arthur thought back to the message he had found aboard The Flounder. Then he remembered Agency Memo 522. Maybe it would be all right after all.

Are they trapped?

87

Agents in Action

Hello shipmates.

As the marine detachment of Action Agents sped towards the pirates, Captain Tar leapt aboard The Flying Fish grinning happily and shouting helloes.

"Captain Tar, how did you..?" began Jim, but he broke off as the boat swung round and headed for the pirates, who had turned tail and scattered over the sea.

The villains tried to sail for safety, but they were no match for the Action Agents. The Flying Fish sped over the waves and rammed the pirates' flagship. Action Agents began to round up waterlogged villains.

Arthur studied each of the captured pirates but there was no sign of Max or Lil. Just then Sleuth growled a warning. Arthur spotted some boats escaping in different directions.

"Max and Lil must be in one of those boats," shouted Kate.

The other agents had their hands full. It was up to Arthur to give chase. He stared at the boats and remembered decoding something about an escape plan.

"Follow me," Arthur yelled, jumping on a handy jetski. "I know which boat they are in."

Which is Max and Lil's boat?

Buried Treasure

Arthur followed the escaping villains. Up ahead he spotted a familiar-looking island and gasped. This was where he and the twins were first marooned.

Arthur jumped off his jetski. He sprinted up the beach then stopped in amazement. Max and Lil were swinging in a large net. Who had caught them?

Just then a tall figure strode out of the jungle. Sleuth wagged his tail happily.

"Uncle Jake!" gasped Arthur.

"Congratulations," he boomed, "Operation Skull and Crossbones has been a great success. Now we must find where these pirates buried their ill-gotten gains."

The captured villains shouted out defiantly. Sleuth barked and tugged at Arthur's pocket. Arthur pulled out a scrap of blue paper. The twins recognized it as Arthur decoded it.

"We know where the loot is," they all yelled. "Come on."

Where is the treasure buried?

90

Clues

You will need to hold this page in front of a mirror to read the clues.

Pages 52-53

Look at the Action Code on page 51.

A = & B = ⇒

Pages 56-57

This is not simple until you get the hang of it. First think backwards, then try swapping the last letter of the first word with the last letter of the next word.

Pages 58-59

Follow the directions in the logbook on the chart.

Pages 60-61

Look carefully at the footprints on the beach.

Pages 62-63

First decode the message on the piece of paper, then use your eyes.

Pages 64-65

Trace over the document fragments then piece them together.

Pages 66-67

Arthur must not touch the coral, but he can scramble over rocks.

Pages 68-69

The key is in the lock on the other side of the door. Is there any way Arthur can reach it?

Pages 70-71

You don't need a clue for this. Just keep your eyes peeled.

Pages 72-73

Read through Bosun Bones' memoirs again.

Pages 74-75

Swap the first word with the third word then swap the fourth word with the sixth word and so on until the end of the message.

Pages 76-77

Plot the course of The Flying Fish and the attack course. Where do they both meet?

Pages 78-79

Avoid any cabins with pirates in them.

Pages 80-81

Look at what the sailors are saying. One nautical mile an hour is one knot.

Pages 82-83

Can they use anything to reflect the sun? Look back to the emergency drill on page 54.

Pages 84-85

This is easy. Use your eyes.

Pages 86-87

Decipher the Agency Memo on page 51 and check the message on page 57.

Pages 88-89

Flick back to the message on page 75. Does it mention an escape plan?

Page 90

Look back at the piece of paper on page 63. What is the final instruction?

Answers

Pages 52-53

The message is written in Action Code. This is what it says:

JOIN THE CREW OF THE FLOUNDER. INVESTIGATE THE DISAPPEARANCE OF SHIPS IN THIS AREA AND PREVENT FURTHER INCIDENTS.

Pages 56-57

The note has been written backwards and the first letter of each word has been swapped with the first letter of the next word. This is what it says with punctuation added:

EMERGENCY: HURRICANE IMMINENT – ALL CAPTAINS INVOLVED WITH OPERATION SKULL AND CROSSBONES ARE ORDERED TO RUN FOR COVER. REGROUP AT ROBA ROBA ISLANDS FLYING CORRECT IDENTIFICATION FLAG.

Pages 58-59

Arthur and the twins are here.

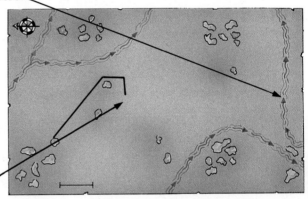

Arthur first works out where they were before the hurricane struck. He does this by plotting their course from the information in the captain's logbook. The course is marked in black. This tells Arthur where they were before the hurricane struck.

The last entry in the logbook tells Arthur that they have been pushed by a north wind at 45 miles an hour. Arthur knows that the hurricane lasted five hours. He works out that they are 225 miles south of their position when the hurricane struck.

This position also ties up with the information the twins have given Arthur, that they are in strong current heading East.

Pages 60-61

Kate has spotted a trail of footprints that does not match any of their footprints.

This trail has been made by someone who is barefoot.

Pages 62-63

Kate and Jim first decode the trail directions on the scrap of paper. They are written backwards with the letter "i" inserted after every three letters. This is what they say:

FROM BUCCANEER BEACH HEAD FOR SKULL ROCK THEN GO EAST THROUGH THE JUNGLE TO GOLDEN BEACH. BURY LOOT SIX FEET UNDER THE EAGLE ROCK.

Jim and Kate then look around and spot a rock with a skull shape carved into it. This must be skull rock where they can pick up the trail.

Pages 64-65

Here is the document after it has been pieced together.

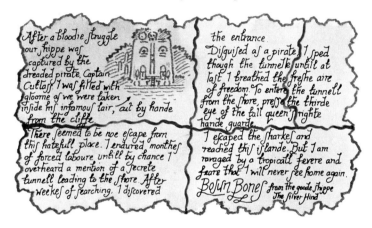

Pages 66-67

The safe route to the boat is marked in black. Although Arthur must not touch the razor-sharp coral, he can scramble over the grey rocks.

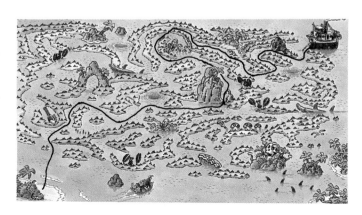

93

Pages 68-69

To escape, Arthur unfolds a newspaper and slides it through the large gap under the door. Next he pushes the key out of the lock with the screwdriver so that the key falls onto the newspaper. Arthur then pulls the newspaper with the key on it back under the door towards him. Once he has the key, he can unlock the door from the inside.

Pages 70-71

Arthur spots several modern details that prove that the galleon is a fake ghost ship.

The giveaway details are ringed in black.

Pages 72-73

Arthur rereads Bosun Bones' memoirs. He realizes that he can get into the base via the secret tunnel that Bosun Bones found. To enter the tunnel, Arthur must press the third eye of the tall queen's right hand guard, here. ———————

Pages 74-75

The message can be decoded by swapping the first word in the message with the third word, the fourth word with the sixth and so on until the end. This is what it says:

SPIDER ORGANIZATION TO MAX MANGLER AND EYE PATCH LIL. WE HAVE THE ROUTE FOR THE NEXT TARGET SHIP, THE FLYING FISH. IT WILL SAIL SW BETWEEN THE SHIP'S GRAVEYARD AND TWIN PEAKS ISLAND UNTIL REACHING THE NORTHERNMOST OF THE THREE NEEDLES. HERE IT WILL TURN AND HEAD NW UNTIL LEVEL WITH EASTERNMOST ISLAND IN THE DIAMOND ARCHIPELAGO. THEN IT WILL CRUISE DUE S BETWEEN SHARK ISLAND AND VOLCANO AND OUT OF OUR TERRITORY. IF AN EMERGENCY OCCURS USE ESCAPE PLAN JPX.

Pages 76-77

The Flying Fish will be attacked in this area.

Arthur works it out by plotting the course of The Flying Fish on the 3-D map. The route of The Flying Fish is marked in red.

Arthur then listens to the instructions that Eye Patch Lil shouts to the pirates. He realizes that The Killer Whale must be the name of the ship that will attack The Flying Fish. The attack course is given in the form of co-ordinates that match areas on the map. Arthur plots this course.

Where the two routes coincide is where The Flying Fish will be attacked.

Pages 78-79

The route up to the deck is marked in black.

Pages 80-81

Arthur knows that he has only six hours to reach The Flying Fish which is 90 nautical miles away. He did some sums based on what the sailors said.

The Turn Turtle only has enough fuel for 80 miles.

The Barnacle would take 7 hours to sail 90 miles.

The Rust Bucket would take 6 hours and 10 minutes to reach The Flying Fish.

The Sea Spray can do 15 knots at top speed. This would reach The Flying Fish in exactly six hours time.

The Sea Spray is the only boat Arthur can take.

Pages 82-83

Arthur can use the mirror or the lenses of the sunglasses to reflect the sun's rays and signal to the ship.

The signals he should use are the ones Captain Tar taught him aboard The Flounder on page 56.

Pages 84-85

Arthur recognizes these two men from the pirate base.

He also notices concealed weapons, a hidden radio and a periscope. They are all ringed in black.

These things convince Arthur that the men on the raft are pirates setting a trap.

Pages 86-87

Arthur realizes that Captain Tar is not a pirate and that they are therefore not trapped.

He works this out after first decoding Agency Memo 522. This says:

IN EMERGENCY ACTION AGENTS MAY TRANSMIT IN SIMPLE CODE. ALL SEABORNE AGENTS ACTIVE IN THIS AREA MUST CARRY BLACK AND RED IDENTIFICATION FLAG.

When Arthur sees Captain Tar and the ships speeding in from starboard, he spots that they are all flying black and red flags. This means that Captain Tar and the others must be Action Agents. Their location ties in with the instructions in the note Arthur found aboard The Flounder on page 57. Because the message was in simple code, not in Agency code, it must have been sent by an Action Agent.

Pages 88-89

Arthur decoded a message on page 75 which mentioned escape plan JPX. When Arthur looks at the getaway boats, he spots one boat with JPX written on it. This is Max and Lil's escape boat.

Page 90

Max and Lil buried their loot under the eagle rock.

This is the final direction on the coded trail written on the blue scrap of paper.

The twins dropped the note when they were captured on page 65. Sleuth gave it to Arthur on pages 66-67.

AGENT ARTHUR'S
ARCTIC ADVENTURE

Martin Oliver

Illustrated by

Paddy Mounter

Designed by
David Gillingwater

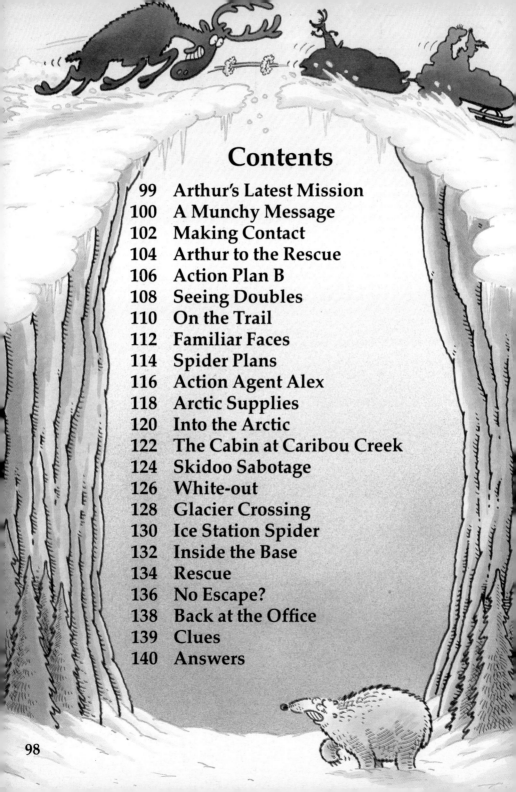

Contents

Arthur's Latest Mission

After his successful mission on the stormy seas, Arthur was looking forward to a well-earned break. But Jake Sharpe, Arthur's uncle, the founder and the brains behind the Action Agency had other ideas.

And so, following Uncle Jake's orders, Arthur soon found himself flying into the Arctic Circle on his latest top-secret mission.

As Arthur flew over icebergs towards the snow-covered coast he tried to remember vital Action Agency information and not to think about holidays.

"Just as well we packed our winter woollies," he whispered to Sleuth. "Still, I'm sure we won't have to go outdoors much. It's far too cold for any villains to be up to no good."

A Munchy Message

Agent Arthur stepped out of the plane in Hudlum Bay, squinting as the sun glared off the snow. He glanced down at Sleuth who snorted in disgust at the blasts of icy wind, then growled at a nearby pack of huskies.

"Come on Sleuth," Arthur shouted. "Let's grab some food."

They slithered across the icy runway, down the main street and into a bar. Arthur quickly ordered, then looked around.

"Hudlum Bay seems normal enough," he thought, above the sound of Sleuth chomping. "I wonder why I was sent here?"

Arthur picked up his moose burger and took a huge bite. A piece of paper flew out of it. Arthur gasped as he spotted some familiar symbols. It was a message from the Action Agency!

What does the message say?

SPECIALITIES
Arctic Roll
Chilli
Polar Beer
Glacier Mince
Ice Burgers
Cold Slaw
Frost Bites
Skate

Making Contact

Arthur retrieved the key from under the iceberg lettuce. He gave Sleuth the note to dispose of, then paid the bill. Sleuth was chewing happily as they left the bar. Keeping alert for skidding skidoos and stray snowballs they headed out into the snowy streets.

They made it safely down Avalanche Avenue and across Polar Bear Boulevard. Arthur pushed open the post office door and strode inside. To his right he saw a row of telephones, and through a door he spotted the left-luggage lockers. Just then a phone began ringing. It was the green one!

Arthur dashed over to it and picked up the receiver. A muffled voice asked a familiar question. It was his contact. Arthur panicked for a second and wished Sleuth wasn't such a quick eater. Then he remembered what to say. He managed to stammer out his reply and waited.

Hello, this is Agent Alex. I'm in a safe house and have information about Spider Organization activities. We'll meet in the park. Hang on, there's a plane right overhead ... OK it's landed. Wait at the fountain SE of the safe house.

Ow!

Arthur listened intently to the agent. His brain reeled in shocked horror at the mention of the Spider Organization, the most powerful gang of criminals in the whole world and sworn enemies of the Action Agency.

Suddenly the voice broke off. Arthur strained his ears. He heard the sounds of a struggle. Then the line went dead.

Arthur stared at Sleuth in horror. A fellow Action Agent was in trouble. Arthur must race to his rescue, but where was Alex? Sleuth barked and scampered off to the lockers. Arthur dashed after him and yanked open locker 13. The Essential Agency Kit fell out. Among the handy objects was a local town plan.

Where should Arthur go?

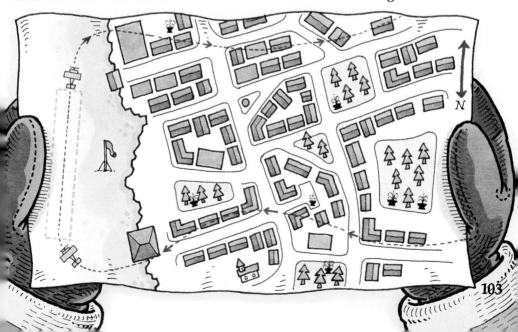

Arthur to the Rescue

Arthur's brain reeled for a second, then he sprang into action. Checking around to make sure no one was watching him, he quickly sorted through the Action Agency equipment and packed it into his backpack.

Arthur grabbed the bag and chased after Sleuth who was racing for the door. They dashed outside, gasping for breath as the cold air hit them. Arthur stepped on a patch of black ice and skidded around a corner.

He careered across the street. Sleuth hardly dared watch as Arthur missed a skidoo and a startled shopper by inches.

As he struggled to stop his slippery slide, Arthur spotted a lamp post. He reached out and clung on desperately.

With Arthur treading carefully and keeping both eyes firmly on the ground, they reached their destination. Arthur studied the large timber house ahead.

"It all seems quiet enough," he whispered. "Maybe we've got the wrong place. I'll try Action Plan A, the direct approach."

He rang the bell and waited . . . and waited. Then he rang again.

At last the door creaked open and a spiky-haired woman stared out at him.

"I'm looking for Alex," Arthur said. "Does he live here?"

The reply seemed innocent enough, but as Arthur turned to go, he realized something was very wrong.

What is wrong?

Action Plan B

Arthur hastily mumbled an apology to the woman, then he and Sleuth walked nonchalantly away until they were out of sight of the house.

"Now for Action Plan B," Arthur hissed. "The sneaky approach."

Keeping to the shadows, they retraced their steps and crept around to the back of the house. Sleuth sniffed the air for danger. It was OK, no one had spotted them. Arthur heard voices inside the house, and, with all senses on red alert, peered in through a grubby window.

He saw the spikey-haired woman and the man from the upstairs window. Arthur's ears pricked up at what he overheard. He whispered a plan to Sleuth who scampered away to trail the burly man.

Who was that?

Just some pesky kid. You join the others with our new hostage, Agent Alex, back at base. I'll search for the information then get back to base. Arrange decoys to put any meddlers off my trail.

You follow the man I'll watch the woman then tail her back to base. We'll meet there.

Arthur looked back into the room and gasped. The woman was methodically ransacking the room. As Arthur watched her closely he thought that she seemed vaguely familiar.

Arthur racked his brains while the woman carried on searching. She grew more and more angry, ripping up floorboards and checking papers and books, but to no avail. Eventually she vaulted out of the window empty handed, aimed a furious karate kick at a water barrel and hurried away.

Just then Arthur remembered a recent Action Agency file. Now he knew who the woman was, but that still left many questions unanswered. If only she had left something that might give Arthur a lead, but she had been too careful.

Or had she?

Seeing Doubles

HUDLUM HARDWARE

Arthur picked up the card. One side was blank, on the flip side were two strangely written words. But there was no time to guess what they meant. Bella was striding away and Arthur musn't lose sight of her.

Arthur raced down the street and into the busy town square. Arthur spotted a woman who looked like Bella. He was about to follow her when he saw another one . . . then another. . . and another.

They were all heading in different directions. Which one should he follow? If only Sleuth were there, he could have sniffed out the real villain from the decoys. But they all looked identical to Arthur.

He stared hard at the women, until in a flash he realized he could work out which one was the real Bella Donna.

Which figure should Arthur follow?

On the Trail

Arthur watched Bella leave the crowded square then he set off through the quiet alleys after her. Tiptoeing silently from building to building, he stalked his quarry through the backstreets of Hudlum Bay.

Arthur tried to melt into the background as his footsteps crunched over the snow. Up ahead Bella stopped. She seemed to be listening for something. Suddenly she whirled around brandishing a gun.

Halt, who goes there? Wha the password?

Minutes later a dark, hairy bundle jumped up at Arthur. It was Sleuth. The two of them hid behind a crate and watched Bella walk up to a canning factory. This must be the crooks' base.

"We've got to get inside," Arthur whispered. "But how can we get past the guard?"

Just then the guard asked Bella for the password.

Arthur dived for cover and held his breath. He looked up. Bella was coming right at him. Just then a black cat darted out in front of Arthur. The villain smiled, lowered her revolver, turned and walked away.

As soon as Arthur's pulse rate returned to normal, he cautiously picked himself up, brushed himself off and started off again. Bella marched on quickly, unaware of the shadowy presence following her.

Pass boss. The rest are waiting inside.

It's me you dummy. OK, the password is . . . mumble . . . mutter.

Arthur couldn't hear her reply, but he noticed the guard checking a card identical to the one Bella had dropped. Arthur realized that the card must be a clue to the password.

As the guard let Bella in, Arthur stared at the card and stepped forward. He was sure he knew the password.

What is the password?

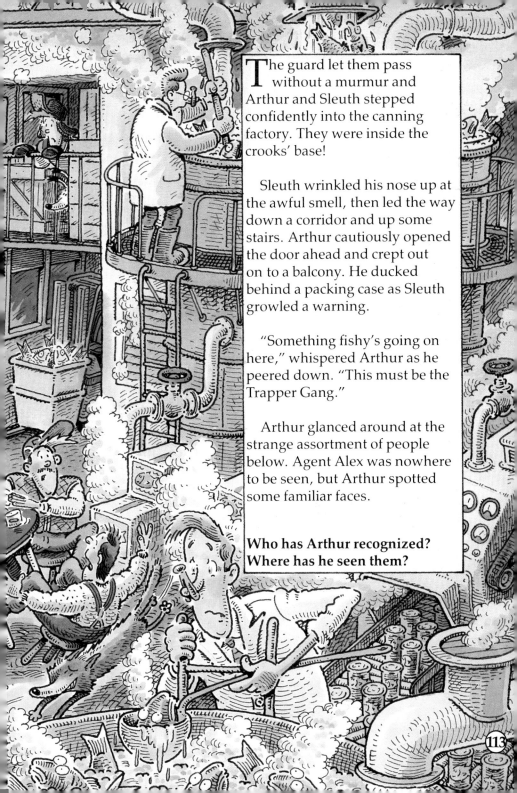

The guard let them pass without a murmur and Arthur and Sleuth stepped confidently into the canning factory. They were inside the crooks' base!

Sleuth wrinkled his nose up at the awful smell, then led the way down a corridor and up some stairs. Arthur cautiously opened the door ahead and crept out on to a balcony. He ducked behind a packing case as Sleuth growled a warning.

"Something fishy's going on here," whispered Arthur as he peered down. "This must be the Trapper Gang."

Arthur glanced around at the strange assortment of people below. Agent Alex was nowhere to be seen, but Arthur spotted some familiar faces.

Who has Arthur recognized? Where has he seen them?

Spider Plans

Where was Agent Alex being held, and what devious plans were these gangsters hatching? Arthur decided to investigate further. Sleuth acted as a lookout while Arthur doubled back, snapped on his flashlight and crept stealthily down a dingy corridor. Up ahead was a door. Arthur stopped, everything seemed quiet. He was just about to try the lock when pain shot up his leg.

"Get off," Arthur hissed until he suddenly realized why Sleuth had stopped him.

Arthur ducked then limped quietly after Sleuth, who led him down another corridor and into an empty office. Sleuth pawed at a locked attache case.

Arthur fumbled with his Agency skeleton key. The lock sprang open. He spread out the contents of the case and stared excitedly at the photos, pictures and writing. Could these be the Spider Organization's plans? He had to decode them.

Can you decipher the codes?

Action Agent Alex

These plans were dynamite! Arthur's brain reeled as he snapped a photo with his Agency mini-camera. His mission now must be to find Ice Station Spider and stop the villains, but what about his contact, the kidnapped Action Agent?

Arthur bundled the plans back into the case. He left the office and began carefully searching the factory. Arthur inched his way down a corridor.

He had just turned left when he heard faint groaning sounds. Where had they come from?

"I don't know who made that noise," hissed Arthur sweeping the area with his flashlight. "But my Action Agent's Instinct tells me that they're in trouble."

Sleuth sniffed the air and wagged his tail. The groaning started again. Arthur stared at the pool of light ahead.

He spotted a figure propped up against a packing case. Arthur recognized his contact in Hudlum Bay. It was Action Agent Alex. He was bound and gagged.

Arthur knelt down and checked that the agent was OK. Alex's eyes opened wide in amazement when he saw Arthur. As Arthur gently peeled off the gag, Alex whispered a vitally important message. When Alex finished, Sleuth began biting through the ropes around his ankles, but the agent stopped him.

"Leave me here," he hissed. "Otherwise those villains will know they've been discovered.

Arthur didn't want to leave his fellow agent in the crooks' clutches, but there was no time to argue. Just then Sleuth growled a warning. He could hear footsteps heading towards them. There was nowhere to run to. They must hide, and quickly.

Where can Arthur and Sleuth hide?

117

Arctic Supplies

Arthur held his breath as the footsteps approached . . . then passed by. Throughout the night he heard shouts and the sounds of things being pushed and dragged around.

It was light before the coast was clear. Arthur nudged Sleuth and they crept out of the case. They dashed out of the deserted factory and back into town. There was no time to lose in getting to the log cabin at Caribou Creek.

"But we can't head off into the icy Arctic wastes," Arthur said, shivering at the thought. "Not until we buy new gear and find Codename Snowstorm."

Arthur flipped through the Agency Handbook. He racked his brains to remember Survival Lesson E for Essential Arctic Equipment, while Sleuth led the way to the shops.

They carefully selected the thickest Arctic gear, and ten layers later they waddled out. Sleuth checked their food supplies while Arthur tested camping equipment.

They staggered out of the ski shop. Arthur hired a souped-up skidoo, test drove it to the garage and filled up the tank and the spare gas cans.

Last of all Arthur bought a sturdy radio. Now they were ready to go, except for one thing; they still hadn't found the undercover Action Agent in town. Arthur thought back to what he had seen and heard. Then he remembered Action Agency Memo 523, and in a sudden flash of inspiration realized who the Agent was.

Who is Codename Snowstorm?

119

Into the Arctic

Arthur and Sleuth skidooed back to the garage where Snowstorm was collecting her sled. Arthur stepped forward and flashed his Action Agency ID. Sleuth wagged his tail as Snowstorm gave the correct Action Agent's reply.

"Search, solve and survive," she whispered. "My name's Zoe, what's going on?"

Zoe listened intently while Arthur explained. As soon as he had finished, Zoe introduced Sleuth to her huskies, hitched up the sled and jumped aboard.

"Follow me," she yelled. "It's a long trek, but I know the way."

They sped off in a cloud of snow. Zoe led the others at breakneck speed over the bleak tundra. She used her natural instincts to guide them deeper and deeper into the freezing wastes, while steering clear of icy hazards and wild animals.

When night fell they set up camp and tried to thaw out by the fire. But it was a sleepless night, and by dawn they were back on the trail. Struggling against exhaustion, they raced over the snow until at last Zoe stopped and pointed to a cabin below. This was Caribou Creek.

The Cabin at Caribou Creek

Sleuth bounded on ahead to sniff out any trouble in the log cabin. He wagged his tail and barked the all-clear to the two agents. Arthur parked the skidoo while Zoe tied up her huskies, then they stepped inside. They glanced around Agent Alex's tidy cabin. Where was the map and the information hidden? The trio began searching.

"With our highly trained Agency skills, this won't take long," Arthur thought confidently.

Just then Zoe cried out. She was holding a large folder. Arthur dashed over and stared at the contents – Action Agency files and papers. They were important, but where was the map that Agent Alex had mentioned?

Agent Angus
special surv_
hang-glidi_

Jane Printz
recent recruit –
ace photographer
– currently working
undercov_ _ Thailand

Captain Jack
Tar
special skills –
surviving stormy seas
latest mission – North Sea
oil rig fire-fighting –
patrol commander

desert

AGENCY
SIGNALS
All signals use
basic equipment
that is readily
available : –
AIR TO GROUND
3 flashes
RED · GREEN · RED =
We will land

GROUND TO AIR
3 flashes
BLUE · GREEN · BLUE =
It's safe to land and
pick us up

SEA TO AIR
GREEN flash =
Make for safety

SEA TO SEA
2 RED flashes = DANGER

1 Arctic HQ
   352 khz
2 Office
   96 fm
3 Pacific HQ
   108 long wave
4 Desert base
   being repaired
5 Island base
   35 fm
6 Jungle hut
   373 khz

CRACK

Zoe and Arthur carried on looking until they slumped dejectedly to the floor.

"Leave that lemming alone," Arthur suddenly shouted to Sleuth. "Or you'll . . ."

Too late. Sleuth crashed into the stove, sending logs flying. One of the logs bounced on the floor and split open. Out rolled a piece of paper.

"It's a Spider Organization map," shouted Zoe. "But what use is it?"

Arthur suddenly remembered the directions he had found in the canning factory. If they followed those directions using this map, he was sure they would locate the Spider Organization's secret Arctic base.

Where is Ice Station Spider?

Skidoo Sabotage

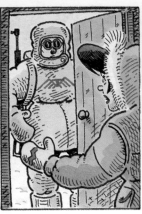

Just then Arthur heard a noise outside. He glanced out of the window and gasped. Armed villains were arriving. It was time to leave, and fast.

Zoe sprang into action as the door opened. She pulled it to, rammed the bolts home then grabbed the map and files.

There was no time to dive for cover as the Spider men opened fire. Bullets whistled through the door into the cabin.

"Our only chance is to stick together and make a break before we're trapped," Arthur shouted. "Follow me."

They dashed out of the back door. Zoe's sled was surrounded. They had to abandon it and sprint for the skidoo.

"All aboard," cried Arthur as the engine roared into life. "Hold on tight, let's go."

The skidoo hurtled away over the snows. Arthur turned to watch the villains disappearing in the distance. He didn't spot the snow drift looming ahead!

It's a bomb.

The Spider Organization's three favorite bombs.

◀ Bomb A
To defuse bomb, disconnect wire joining two of the green terminals.

Bomb B ▶
To make bomb safe, cut the wires connecting the green terminals to each other.

◀ Bomb C
Defuse bomb by cutting wire that connects a green to a yellow terminal.

Zoe managed to throw herself clear as Arthur and Sleuth were catapulted head first into the powdery snow. Zoe got groggily to her feet. She began making her way towards the muffled cries for help when something on the chassis of the upturned skidoo caught her eye.

She gasped in horror. It was a bomb! So that was why the villains had let them escape.

"Take cover," mumbled Arthur, burrowing deeper into the snow.

"But we must save the skidoo. It's all we have left since those villains captured my huskies and sled," sniffed Zoe.

She opened her Action Agency Handbook. First she must identify the bomb, then defuse it.

Can you defuse the bomb?

White-out

Zoe held her breath as she cut the wire. The bomb stopped ticking. She let out a huge sigh of relief and stowed the bomb in her pack. Arthur dug himself out of the snow drift and checked their essential survival equipment. The everything-proof unbreakable radio was broken! Arthur assessed their situation.

"There's a direct route to Ice Station Spider," Zoe said, once he had finished. "But it will be a long hard journey across the bleak Arctic wastes. We must start right now."

Zoe was right. Arthur snapped on his snow goggles. He started the skidoo and the trio headed off. As they drove into the empty white landscape, Arthur shivered. Would they ever see Hudlum Bay again?

For four days and nights they struggled on, pitting their wits and Action Agency skills against the treacherous terrain and hostile climate. Biting winds froze their flesh. The trio stretched their limbs to breaking point as they hauled themselves over icy obstacles and escaped from angry Arctic animals.

At the end of the fifth day, they set up camp on the icecap. Zoe studied the map. They had made good progress northward, now maybe it was time to head East. While Zoe was checking their position, Arthur peered out of the tent and spotted some wreckage in the distance.

"I'll investigate that crashed chopper due West," Arthur said, trying to stop his teeth from chattering. "Come on, Sleuth."

Be careful. I think there's a storm brewing.

Sleuth reluctantly trailed after Arthur. The wind blew away Zoe's warning. Arthur and Sleuth trudged on and on in a straight line towards the helicopter. The wind started howling and thick snow swirled around them.

"We must get back to the tent," Arthur shouted as gusts of wind blasted towards them, driving blinding snow into their eyes. "We'll never survive this weather in the open."

But as they retraced their steps, the tent disappeared in the white-out conditions. Arthur huddled next to Sleuth for warmth. He emptied out his pockets and suddenly realized they had a chance to get back.

What can Arthur use?
How can they get back?

Glacier Crossing

Arthur and Sleuth had thawed out by dawn when Zoe struck camp. They headed East and glided along smoothly until the skidoo shuddered, spluttered and died. They were out of gas.

"It doesn't matter," said Zoe, pointing down. "We've made it to the Fox's Glacier, but this is where the going gets really tough. From now on we must go by foot. We'll only take what we can carry."

THIN ICE

Sadly they abandoned the skidoo and sorted through their gear. Arthur staggered under the weight of his backpack, then he gritted his teeth and stared down defiantly.

They had to cross the glacier, despite the deadly crevasses, wild animals and thin ice.

Can you find a safe route across the glacier?

129

Ice Station Spider

The gentle slope on the other side of the glacier soon became an uphill struggle. Numb with cold, the trio scrabbled for a grip on the slippery ice.

At last they reached the top. Zoe peered through the mist. Ice Station Spider was somewhere in the valley below. They must get down for a closer look, but how?

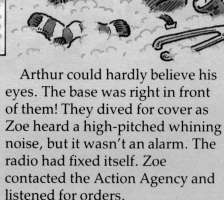

Suddenly an ominous crack broke the silence and the ground collapsed from under them. Arthur, Zoe and Sleuth bounced and rolled down onto solid pack ice. Their equipment avalanched down the slope and landed around them.

Arthur could hardly believe his eyes. The base was right in front of them! They dived for cover as Zoe heard a high-pitched whining noise, but it wasn't an alarm. The radio had fixed itself. Zoe contacted the Action Agency and listened for orders.

Well done Agents. Your orders are to enter the base, recover the germ bombs and release the hostages. We will be overhead in four hours to collect you.

"Getting in should be easy," said Arthur confidently. "That fence will never stop highly trained Action Agents like us."

"That's no ordinary fence," replied Zoe. "It's electric, and carrying a lethal load."

Arthur gulped. How would they get past the killer fence? Just then Sleuth chased off after an Arctic fox. Arthur sighed. This was no time for games. He began studying the equipment nearby.

How can they get into the base?

Inside the Base

Arthur and Zoe squeezed after Sleuth. Zoe held the torch while Arthur enlarged the tunnel with an ice pick. It was slow work, but at last they crawled up to the surface and wriggled out. They were inside the base.

Just then a searchlight swept over the ground towards them. Zoe dived back into the tunnel as Arthur and Sleuth flattened themselves face down into the snow. The searchlight passed silently over them.

Action Agents here! Go and guard the hostages, you three come with me.

Boss, we've found a tunnel leading into the base, with an Action Agency Handbook in it.

While Zoe was planting the 'diversion', Arthur and Sleuth watched Bella lock away the last deadly germ bomb. The safe door had just clanged shut when a mean-looking guard rushed into the hut shouting.

Arthur gasped. The tunnel had been discovered, but what about Zoe? Bella Donna punched an alarm button on the desk and barked orders to her henchmen. A siren began to wail as the crooks raced out of the hut.

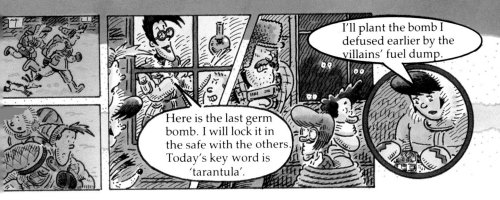

The agents leapt into action. Keeping to the shadows, they darted through the camp, checking buildings and dodging guards. They peered in through the windows of two adjacent huts and grinned triumphantly.

At last they had found the germ bombs and the hostages. First they must get the bombs.

"We need a diversion," said Zoe smiling. "And I've got just the thing."

Arthur broke into the hut and raced over to the safe. It would be easy to open, he knew the key word. But the console buttons were numbered! How could he tap in letters? Just then Zoe appeared beside him.

She began checking the papers on the desk and the walls. Arthur joined her. Maybe they contained a clue. It was a long shot, but they had to take it.

How can they open the safe?

133

Rescue

The safe door swung open. Trying to stop their hands shaking, Arthur and Zoe began gingerly picking up the phials containing the deadly germs and placing them gently in a steel box. At last the safe was empty. Now they must release the hostages, but what about their guards?

"I've got something up my sleeve for them," whispered Arthur, producing a knockout gas grenade. "It's quick-working and has no lasting side effects."

"Great idea," said Zoe, as they crept outside. "But what's happened to my diversion."

Just then an enormous BANG echoed through the camp. Zoe smiled. That should keep the villians busy.

Arthur tried the door to the hostage hut. It was unlocked. He and Zoe tied scarves round their faces then Arthur lobbed the grenade into the hut.

Five seconds later the Action Agents followed. They were just in time to see the guards slump to the floor, asleep. Sleuth disarmed them while Zoe and Arthur untied the dopey hostages, hauled them out of the hut and locked the door behind them.

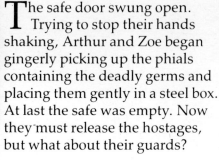

Agent Alex and Professor Tube soon came to in the cold. They stared around in amazement. Ice Station Spider was in chaos. The fuel dump was ablaze and gang members were racing around trying to put out the fire. They were too busy to notice the agents and the freed hostages.

Suddenly Sleuth's ears pricked up. Above the roar of the flames he could hear an engine. He barked at the others and they stared upwards. Arthur spotted a dark shape hovering in the sky.

"It's an Agency helicopter," he shouted. "We're saved."

"But it's not landing," Zoe yelled.

Zoe was right, and Arthur suddenly realized why. The chopper needed landing signals. Arthur racked his brains. He knew where to get the signals, but what were the correct ones?

Where can Arthur find signals? Which ones should he use?

No Escape?

A rthur ducked under the rotor blades and jumped into the helicopter, seconds before it roared up into the sky.

"Mission accomplished," Arthur yelled as he saw the germ bombs and everyone safely aboard.

"Not yet," boomed a familiar voice from the cockpit.

Arthur gasped as the pilot turned round, smiling. It was Uncle Jake!

ESCAPE ROUTES
TO BE COVERED

Gate 1 —
Gate 2 —
Gate 3 —
Rocket —
Helicopter —
Skidoos —
Any other way out?

"Detachments of back-up agents have landed to round up the villains," he said, handing Arthur a piece of paper. "As you know the situation on the ground, I want you to check that we've covered all possible escape routes out of the base."

Arthur stared at the list and peered down at the chaotic scene below. The Agency seemed to have all the routes covered.

Have they?

Back at the Office

But remember that we must never relax our efforts to solve mysteries and to defeat the Spider Organization.

A rthur was proudly clutching the Agency's highest award, the Action Arrow, presented by Uncle Jake. Arthur looked round happily at the familiar faces.

As he listened to Uncle Jake's speech his mind flashed back to the Arctic operation against Ice Station Spider. The back-up agents had found the tunnel in time to catch all the villains.

Except one. Bella Donna had managed to slip through their fingers. Suddenly Arthur's spine tingled. He sensed that someone was watching, and he had a feeling he knew who it was. This time there would be no escape. Arthur tensed himself, ready to spring into action...

Who's watching Arthur?

Clues

You will need to hold this page in front of a mirror to read the clues.

Pages 100-101

Look back to the Action Code on page 99. A = §   B = π

Pages 102-103

What did Agent Alex say? Look closely at the town plan.

Pages 104-105

Think carefully about the woman's reply.

Pages 106-107

This is easy. Use your eyes.

Pages 108-109

Compare the figures that look like Bella with the real Bella on pages 106-107.

Pages 110-111

Where is the word "in" in relation to the word "out".

Pages 112-113

This is easy. Check the characters that appear earlier in the book.

Pages 114-115

There are two different codes. Try thinking backwards for one and swapping the first and last letters of each word for the other.

Pages 116-117

This is easy.

Pages 118-119

Decode Memo 523 on page 99.

Pages 122-123

Look back to the coded directions on page 115.

Pages 124-125

Look carefully at the electrical circuits for each bomb in the Handbook. Which one matches the bomb on the skidoo?

Pages 126-127

Arthur set off in a straight line due West away from the tent. In what direction must they travel to get back to it?

Pages 128-129

You don't need a clue for this.

Pages 130-131

Is there a way under the fence?

Pages 132-133

Look closely at all the pieces of paper on the walls and on the desk. One of them has the first four letters of the key word written on it.

Pages 134-135

Look at the Agency Signals on page 122, and check the buildings in the base on pages 130-131.

Pages 136-137

How did Arthur get into the base?

Page 138

This is easy. Use your eyes.

Answers

Pages 100-101

The message is written in Action Code. This is what it says:

PROCEED TO POST OFFICE. ANSWER GREEN PHONE. CONTACT WILL ASK IS THE BAKED ALASKA READY. REPLY YES IT WILL BE RIGHT ON TIME. AGENCY KIT IN LOCKER 13. KEY UNDER LETTUCE.

Pages 102-103

Arthur should go to the safe house.

The safe house is here.

It is the only house with the landing flight path directly overhead and a fountain in a park to the South East.

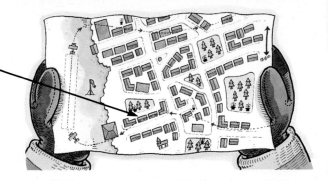

Pages 104-105

Arthur thinks logically about the woman's reply and realizes that she is lying. If she knew he had rung twice, either she had heard the first ring, or someone must have told her. Arthur also spots a face at the upstairs window.

Pages 106-107

Bella has dropped this piece of paper.

Pages 108-109

This is the real Bella Donna. The others are all wearing slightly different clothes.

No hood.

Wrong grip on boots.

Different colour jacket.

Different colour boots.

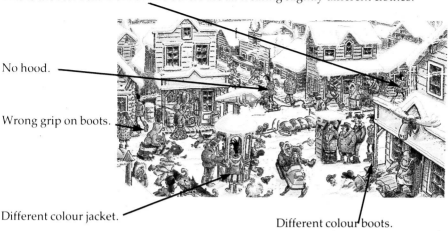

Pages 110-111

Arthur notices that the word "in" is written on its side, and that it is also inside the middle letter of the word "out".

Thinking laterally, he realizes that the password is 'Inside Out'.

Pages 112-113

Arthur recognizes four people from the town square on pages 108-109.

Pages 114-115

The code on the piece of paper with the Spider logo can be deciphered by swapping the first and last letters of each word. This is what it says with punctuation added:

YOU CAN'T FLY DIRECTLY TO BASE DUE TO MOUNTAINS AND SNOWSTORMS. YOU MUST FOLLOW THE SPIDER ROUTE. FLY NORTH TO FIRST BEACON THEN TURN EAST TO THE SEA. CARIBOU CREEK IS DUE WEST. CONTINUE NORTH TO SECOND BEACON. BELOW BEACON IS A VILLAGE. AT THE VILLAGE FLY WEST THROUGH VALLEY TO THIRD BEACON, THEN SOUTH TOWARDS BEACON NUMBER FOUR. BELOW BEACON IS A GLACIER. FOLLOW THE GLACIER NW TOWARDS THE FIFTH BEACON. THE BASE IS IN THE VALLEY ON THE EAST SIDE OF THE MOUNTAIN SE OF THE LAST BEACON.

Pages 114-115 (continued)

Each paragraph on the pink pad of paper has been written backwards with spaces inserted irregularly between letters. This is what it says:

SPIDER ORGANIZATION WORLD DOMINATION PLAN 3.

PHASE 1. BELLA DONNA AND THE TRAPPER GANG TO BUILD SECRET BASE IN REMOTE PART OF ARCTIC. BASE TO BE CALLED ICE STATION SPIDER. COMPLETED.

PHASE 2. BELLA TO KIDNAP SCIENTIST PROFESSOR TESS TUBE AND FORCE HER TO WORK AT ICE STATION SPIDER. ENGINEERS TO CONSTRUCT SPIDER ROCKET. COMPLETED.

PHASE 3. PROFESSOR TUBE WILL MAKE LETHAL GERM BOMBS FOR OUR ROCKET. BELLA TO WIND UP ACTIVITIES IN HUDLUM BAY THEN RETURN TO GUARD ICE STATION SPIDER. ONCE THE BOMBS ARE FINISHED WE WILL HOLD THE WORLD TO RANSOM AND DEMAND TOTAL GLOBAL CONTROL.

Pages 116-117

This is the only place where Arthur and Sleuth can hide.

Pages 118-119

This is Codename Snowstorm.

> Come back in half an hour. Your green sled will be fixed then.

Arthur works this out by thinking back to Action Agency Memo 523 on page 99. When decoded it says:

WHEN WRITTEN, ALL AGENTS' CODENAMES MUST APPEAR AS ANAGRAMS WITH NUMBERS IN REVERSE ORDER.

Arthur realizes that the address written on the side of the green sled is an anagram of Snowstorm, and that 132 is Snowstorm's number written backwards.

The owner of the green sled must be Codename Snowstorm. When Arthur overhears the mechanic he realizes who the sled's owner is.

Pages 122-123

Arthur remembers the directions he decoded on page 115.

He follows them on the map. The route is marked in black.

Ice Station Spider is here.

Caribou Creek is here.

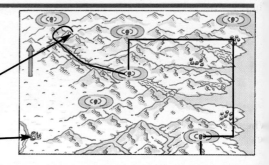

Pages 124-125

The bomb planted on the skidoo has the same electrical circuit as Bomb C in the Handbook. To defuse it, Zoe must cut this wire.

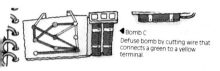

◀ Bomb C
Defuse bomb by cutting wire that connects a green to a yellow terminal.

Pages 126-127

Arthur and Sleuth set off from the tent, walking in a straight line towards the crashed chopper. Before they reach it, they are forced to turn back and begin to retrace their steps before stopping.

They walked due West towards the chopper, so Arthur realizes they must head due East to get back to the tent. To plot this course, Arthur must use the compass he has turned out of his pocket.

Pages 128-129

The safe route across the glacier is marked in black.

Pages 130-131

There is a tunnel that leads under the fence and into the base. This is Arthur's way in.

When Sleuth chases after the Arctic fox he enters the tunnel here.

The Arctic fox is running out of the tunnel here.

Pages 132-133

This piece of paper shows the first four letters of the key word with numbers written below them.

Arthur realizes that each letter in the alphabet is represented by a different number. He also suspects that there is a pattern to the code.

He knows from the paper that A = 12, so he continues this pattern where B = 13, C = 14 and so on until O = 26. When he reaches P, he goes back to number 1 then continues Q = 2, R = 3, S = 4, T = 5 and on until he reaches Z. This fits in with the letters and numbers on the piece of paper

Arthur then reads off the numbers that represent each letter of the key word 'TARANTULA'.

To open the safe he punches in these numbers: 5, 12, 3, 12, 25, 5, 6, 23, 12.

Pages 134-135

Arthur can find signalling equipment in the hut right beside him.

These are the correct Agency signals.

Zoe found them in Agent Alex's log cabin on page 122.

Pages 136-137

The Action Agency haven't covered the tunnel that Arthur and Zoe used to enter the base.

Page 138

Bella Donna is watching from the window.

You can also spot some familiar faces from Arthur's earlier adventures.

First published in 1991 by
Usborne Publishing Ltd,
Usborne House,
83-85 Saffron Hill,
London EC1N 8RT, England

Copyright © 1991 Usborne Publishing Ltd.

The name Usborne and the device ♥ are
Trade Marks of Usborne Publishing Ltd.

Printed in Italy.   American edition